THIS IS A BLACKCURRANT PRESS PUBLICATION

Adventures of a Thought Thief Part II

A Calling to Courage - the challenge

Written by Beverly A. Burchett

ISBN # 979-8-9882754-1-1

Printed in the United States of America

Dedication

To my nieces and nephews who are as smart as they are strong and brave. My love for them is like the size of the ocean - vast, and immeasurable.

Adventures of a Thought Thief

Part II

A Calling to Courage - the challenge

Written by Beverly A. Burchett

CHAPTER 1. Princess Asha had to be carried to her chamber that evening. Naturally, she was too distraught over her brother's abduction to walk. The timing of her collapse did not draw any suspicion, although it occurred directly after she was rigorously questioned by her father, King Degnal, about her own kidnapping and mysterious return.

"I demand that you tell me immediately the names of the conspirators who whisked you away so many moons ago from my kingdom!" King Degnal shouted at her.

All King Degnal received from his daughter, Asha, that evening was the sight of her collapsing to the floor. The palace Khem it, Elimu, was summoned instantaneously, and King Degnal angrily retreated to his throne, thoroughly unsatisfied. King Degnal knew now that he should have insisted his daughter permit him to seek revenge on her abductors. Instead, he let her talk him out of it, saying that she was drugged and couldn't remember all events with any clarity. He regretted that moment of weakness. His daughter's safe return impeded his kingly duties. Some believed that had King Degnal pursued his daughter's captors, they would not have even thought to take his son.

Elimu quickly arrived at Princess Asha's chamber and prepared and administered a strong potion for her, his special sleep-inducing tea of passion flower and chamomile.

Asha sipped the brew, and soon began to doze off in her chair by the fire. Kena was so worried about her mistress that she would not leave her side, but lowered herself down at Asha's feet. Meanwhile, Elimu collected his remedies and exited, having accomplished his task.

Once the Khem it was gone and all was quiet in the palace hallway surrounding Asha's chamber, the Princess suddenly bolted upright in her seat. Kena was so startled, she nearly yelled out. But Asha swiftly placed her finger across her lips and gestured that Kena not make a sound. Kena caught on quickly, and raced over to the door to make sure it was securely latched. When she returned to Asha's side, the two silently giggled uncontrollably.

"My, my Mistress, you are a clever one…" Kena whispered "…How did you manage the brew?"

"I spit it back into the cup, of course," Princess Asha informed her.

"Ah…" Kena replied with a smile.

Kena realized that she should have known. Princess

Asha had become somewhat of an expert at hiding her pregnancy right in plain sight. When Princess Asha experienced her morning sicknesses, Kena hardly noticed her vomiting her meal back onto the platter. Princess Asha made it seem as if she ate something that disagreed with her. And when Asha's clothing tugged against her increasingly swelling middle section, Princess Asha would stand at particular angles to show her body in a more flattering light. With simple pleats and sashes, she managed to look every bit the young daughter of a King, and not the soon to be young mother. So far, no one suspected her of being with child except for her seamstress, Amma Khan. She knew even before anything began to show. It was clear to both Princess Asha and Kena that Amma Khan was a complete wonder and not just with fabrics and designs.

Suddenly, Kena stared at her Mistress with a stream of concern upon her face.

"What?" Princess Asha asked.

"Will this really work?" Kena asked.

"Ah, so that is the worry I see on your face…" Princess Asha replied, "…No need. Not only will this work, it will save this Kingdom."

With a triumphant turn, Princess Asha walked over

to the fire and emptied the rest of the content in her cup into it. Kena immediately jumped up to take the dirty vessel from her Mistress' hand.

"He's a peevish, selfish runt who will be missed by no one!" Princess Asha nearly screamed.

Immediately, the Degnal Guards tapped on the chamber door thinking the Princess was in distress.

"Mistress?" one of the Guards asked.

"I'm fine," Princess Asha reassured them.

Kena didn't wish to argue with her Mistress, but they had just left the King's presence and he was at least one who appeared greatly disturbed by the news of his son, Oban's disappearance. In fact, he bellowed shamelessly in agony and then demanded everyone leave his sight. Had it not been for Princess Asha fainting, he would have thrown her out too.

"I know what you are thinking, Kena…" Princess Asha said, "…Yes, my Father King will miss the little toad, but in time, in time, he shall receive a new son…a greater son…my son."

"Brilliant, Mistress," Kena exclaimed.

"It is, isn't it? Pity I didn't think of it myself…" Princess Asha agreed, "…I will have to thank the one who did as soon as our paths cross…" she said contemplatively, "…First, my Father King will fall into the same melancholy as he had during my long absence…" she said.

"He was very distressed and ran out looking for you far and wide," Kena said.

"…I believe he will do the same for his son, the dog, and…" Princess Asha smiled.

"And?" Kena asked.

"…And when he returns this time, road weary and empty handed, I shall deliver to him a prize…a new Prince for his Kingdom," Princess Asha said joyfully.

"It will warm his heart!" Kena exclaimed with glee.

"It will…" Princess Asha smiled, "…and I will be the savior for him. He will not suffer one day of shame for not having a male heir on the throne. Unlike my Queen Mother, who is too old to do so, I will provide another for him."

Princess Asha leaned back in her seat and grinned blissfully. Kena sat beneath her and began rubbing her feet. Neither could believe their good fortune at Prince Oban's disappearance. Now, with King Degnal preoccupied traipsing all over the Great Lands to find him, Princess Asha's pregnancy would assuredly continue to go unnoticed.

Kenneth Kingdom, northern Great Lands

CHAPTER 2. Kenneth was known for its brittle cold weather, but that was especially true at its northernmost peaks. As the Elders stood atop one of its highest mountains, their exhaled breath froze in midair. No form of animal skin could keep the bitter chill from their aging bones. None seemed to mind though as they waited anxiously for their impending fate of the spell cast by Priest Godlumthakathi. They all knew that there was a price to pay. Unfortunately, one of them would have to give up their very life to satisfy the debt.

Priest Godlumthakathi was purposely prolonging his entrance to the gathering. He had yet to receive the Elders' selected sacrifice. So, he languidly labored below continuing to assemble the preparations. Though the Elders had vowed to let him know in plenty of time, as the sun set, they still had not made their choice.

Finally, Priest Godlumthakathi made the long trek up the mount carrying all the necessary effects for the ritual. They were few; peppermint leaves to sprinkle on the fire of the deceased remains, and a thick blade to chop off the honoree's head. Kennethians would sing a traditional dirge throughout the ceremony intended to release the deceased's spirit into the arms of the Kenneth gods. The skull, once removed of its flesh, would then be carried on the silver plate specifically reserved for the occasion. It would remain in the village center so all from near and far could pay tribute until the next new moon.

"Greetings, Priest Godlumthakathi," Elder Isoba said, as the Priest made his appearance onto the summit.

Priest Godlumthakathi nodded to all present but did not speak. Out of necessity, he was preserving his energy. He'd require every bit of it in order to perform the rites. Each incantation had to be precise so that the deceased's journey could go about smoothly into the great beyond.

The Elders gave the Priest plenty of room as he went about cleaning the altar. He took his time scrubbing it down with a mixture of water and salt. Next, he removed a monstrously sharp knife from its sheath and washed it also in the same manner. It took the Elders aback when they saw it, as it gleamed in the evening light, but they remained calm. Each said a secret prayer hoping their neck would not come into contact with its edge.

After the cleansing tasks were completed, Priest Godlumthakathi would insist upon the Elder's choice. Knowing this, the Elders quickly huddled together to discuss the matter one last time.

"Has anyone anything new to add?" Elder Isoba tiredly, asking his fellow weary brothers, "...We've been up here since first light and have not made much progress."

Everyone shook their head, "no" to his question then stood silently reserved.

"It didn't even work…" Elder Nafari said, "…How can we still be responsible for a failed spell?"

All of the Elders nodded their heads in agreement. In hushed tones, they expressed their displeasure with what they determined was the Priest's ineffective magic.

"Nafari is correct…" Elder Sam told them, "…If the butcher doesn't chop the meat, he is not paid. Excuse the analogy…" he paused, "…And, if a jeweler does not set a stone, he receives no reward. And, if a baker…"

"Yes, yes, Sam…" Elder Duna interrupted, "…We are quite aware of how these transactions work."

"As I've been saying, it did not work," Elder Nafari reiterated.

All of the Elders nodded in agreement again.

"I do not wish to wrestle with the Priest, but someone must tell him that he isn't due, how did you say it, Sam, a reward," Elder Duna said.

The Elders lowered their head in thought and then one by one they began to focus their attention on Elder Isoba.

"Why me?" he asked, "Because I am the eldest of the Elders?"

"Well…" Elder Sam began.

"You are the wisest…" Elder Duna told him, "…I'm looking at you because I hope you have something in mind besides this bloody business."

"Flattery will not work…" Elder Isoba said, "…Not this time anyway."

"Are there any among us who wish to volunteer?" Elder Duna asked the group.

The Elders hung their heads on their chests without replying to Elder Duna's question. They were all thinking the same thing, if they confronted the Priest, he would make them the sacrifice. Elder Isoba sighed, summoning courage as he exhaled, then moved toward the Priest.

Priest Godlumthakathi did not appear surprised at his approach, but fanned his arm round gesturing Elder Isoba kneel before the altar. Elder Isoba raised his chin and eyed the Priest for a few moments before speaking.

"Priest Godlumthakathi, I have something that I

would like to suggest…" Elder Isoba said as a request.

Priest Godlumthakathi merely nodded for Elder Isoba to continue. Ordinarily, no discussion was made at this time, but Priest Godlumthakathi felt obligated to appease the eldest of the Elders. He had known him his entire life, and like everyone else in the Kenneth, considered him a father figure. By now, all of the Elders were standing near the altar.

"Priest Godlumthakathi, I'll say this diplomatically as I can…" Elder Isoba began, "…We…I…feel that a breach has taken place with this exchange and, therefore, our end of the bargain cannot be delivered.

Priest Godlumthakathi eyed the Elder suspiciously for a few moments and then scanned his gaze around to each and every elder present. He had not seen this tactic coming and wasn't prepared for it.

"Yes?" he spoke for the first time, inquiring about the specifics of Elder Isoba's argument.

"It didn't work!" shouted Elder Sam, followed by a unanimous, "Aye," from the other Elders.

"Those Degnal soldiers were clever, yes…" Priest Godlumthakathi said.

"They were more than clever. They outwitted our

fiercest magic!" Elder Nafari huffed.

"This is why we do not owe a life today because, in every practical way, the magic did not work," Elder Isoba concluded.

"It didn't work?" Priest Godlumthakathi asked.

"No," Elder Isoba answered.

"How do we know that it didn't work?" Priest Godlumthakathi asked, "None of us were there."

"If it had done its job, the Degnalites would be groveling at our feet, scared of us because we look like giants to them. Instead, they are in celebration of their triumph over Kenneth…" Elder Isoba went on.

The Elders felt embolden as he spoke and offered words of agreement and encouragement, but kept their distance from the Priest.

"…Should we be responsible to the gods for services that have not been rendered?" Elder Isoba inquired.

"No," Priest Godlumthakathi simply said.

"Well…" Elder Isoba said, "…That was easier than I imagined…" he looked over at the other Elders, "…It appears no one is dying today!"

The Elders lifted up a shout of joy, while Priest Godlumthakathi removed all of his props from on and around the altar. The Elders were already facing the pathway leading down from the mountain when Priest Godlumthakathi called out to them.

"Elders, you have forgotten one thing…" he told them.

The Elders turned apprehensively to face the Priest again.

"What?" Elder Isoba asked.

"Well, the spell is still at hand and we must utilize it on our enemy, or our brethren before the next new moon, less we all die…" Priest Godlumthakathi informed and then warned them, "…Your choice, one today or all on the second light."

"I knew we should not have practiced dark magic…" Elder Duna swore, "…It never ends well."

CHAPTER 3. Asha sat comfortably in her seat at supper that evening, patiently waiting for the announcement from her King father. It wouldn't be long. The main course had already been cleared from the table and the King's guests were happily lounging, having eaten their bounty of rich food. The musicians would play all night at the King's request, of course, and they chimed on incessantly to Asha's annoyance. Indeed, the general merriment continually distracted her from her purpose. Come what may though, she would not miss a single moment of this delicious intrigue that was about to unfold before her. She was certain that at any moment, the chamber's gaiety would abruptly halt and Commander Testlar and her King father would go riding off into the night air in search of the little peevish menace, her brother.

However, as the night dragged on, Asha grew increasingly impatient wondering why on earth they hadn't departed. As she continued to observe her King father, he didn't even seem as if he had any intention of moving at all. He hadn't dismissed the beverage server, and it was doubtful he ever would. By her count, he was just finishing his third goblet of beer. She now watched anxiously as he drained the last gulp. To her disappointment, he simply turned and requested another. It was not in his character to do so. He was a light drinker always preferring to feign drunkenness than to actually be absent from his wits.

Asha turned away quickly, lest he caught her scrutinizing his every move. She wanted to sulk but decided she had better at least appear somewhat joyful despite the delay in the King's pronouncement. Fortunately, to her delight, she was able to eat normally, now that her pregnancy sickness was at an end. She had almost forgotten the taste of millet and honey. The sweetness tickled her belly and made the baby kick. It startled her at first and nearly made her squeal with pleasure. She kept her composure though and allowed herself to smile on the inside. She couldn't wait to meet the new prince. She was so looking forward to giving birth.

As Asha grinned within her heart over the future of Degnal, she saw Guedado, one of the King's guards, glancing in her direction. She knew that he was fond of her and when it suited her purposes, she'd sometimes entertain his foolhardy delusions.

"Princess, Asha, you're practically glowing,"

Guedado expressed brightly to her as he approached.

It was not unusual for him to speak to her in such a familiar manner and yet she still felt as if it was an affront. After all, he wasn't even a high-ranking guard. If it were Commander Testlar commenting on her appearance, she wouldn't have flinched or wished that he would fall to his knees and bowed before her.

"Thank you, Guedado," she managed through gritted teeth.

In fact, she was just about to dismiss him when she suddenly thought of some use for him. She lowered her head and bade he come closer into her confidence. Guedado eagerly rushed to Asha's side and leaned over to hear and to readily fulfill her every desire. His loathsome gushing notwithstanding, Asha spoke.

"Surely you hear all sorts of things throughout the Kingdom?" Asha began.

"Yes, my Princess…" Guedado replied proudly, "…It is my duty as one of the King's guards to know what is going on within his realm."

"Yes, of course. I knew you were the right man," Asha smiled attempting something resembling flattery.

"At your service, my Princess," Guedado beamed.

Then he knelt down respectfully and awaited orders from his Princess. Asha smiled, enjoying his immediate obedience. She enjoyed watching her servants indulge her every whim.

"Will you be leaving at first light?" Asha asked coyly.

"My Princess?" Guedado asked, confused about her question.

"In search of the Prince, of course," Asha explained.

"Princess Asha, the main gate is closed for the night," Guedado informed her.

Asha stared at Guedado for several moments carefully processing his words. They both knew that once the gate was down, no one was allowed outside of it. 'How could that be?' Asha wondered. 'Is the King not searching for my brother after all?' she thought. Then she glanced over at her King father and couldn't believe what she was witnessing. At that precise moment, the King was busily requesting yet another drink, this time of wine. The wine steward poured the liquid into his goblet all the way up to the brim. Then the royal taster took a sip, waited a goodly length of time, and then placed the vessel into the King's hand, and he did drink.

"We are all worried about the Prince, Princess Asha," Guedado said in the most touching way he could muster.

Asha nearly laughed at his concern for the boy, but luckily caught herself before her face gave away her true sentiments. She could no more be worried about Oban, her brother, than she could be for the mangy dogs in the Degnal forest. Her only concern was keeping her King father preoccupied long enough for her to produce the newest member of the Degnal family, the rightful heir to the throne, her son.

"Thank you, Guedado," Asha muttered, dismissing him briskly.

Guedado regretfully rose and hesitantly backed away from Princess Asha. He couldn't believe his good fortune to have been so long in her presence. He nearly stumbled as if in a trance, but caught hold of himself just in time.

As he traversed through the throngs of people back to his station, he got an inspired thought that could possibly bring him back to his Princess. Before he knew it, he was marching toward the King. Before he could reach him though, Commander Testlar immediately blocked his way and now stood menacingly over him.

"Commander," Guedado saluted.

Commander Testlar merely nodded back without saying a word.

"Pardon my intrusion, Sir…" Guedado said shyly, perceptively realizing that he would not be permitted an audience with the King any time soon.

Commander Testlar raised his head in the direction of Guedado's station, and then squinted angrily at him to retreat back to it.

"Yes, Sir…of course, Sir…" Guedado stammered, "…I merely wished to know…for the sake of the Princess, who is worried…Will we ride tonight to look for the Prince, Sir?" he finally asked.

Commander Testlar immediately looked over at Princess Asha, who was at that exact moment staring at her father, the King, then he returned his gaze to Guedado. With pure intimidation, he waited a lengthy time before he even addressed him. Guedado felt uncomfortable and nearly walked away from the strength of that feeling. Finally, Commander Testlar replied by simply saying, "No."

CHAPTER 4. Unbeknownst to his kidnappers, Oban, son of King Degnal, had been awake since first light. He was trying to quickly assess his situation that he knew was dire. He immediately sent word to his father, King Degnal, informing him that he had been abducted in the middle of the night while he slept. He managed this communication, of course, through the power of thought. This method for delivering a message had worked well before when King Runmari tried to invade Degnal Kingdom. Back then, he entered the mind of his father and placed a thought in it, a cry for help. Before dawn, his father rode to his rescue. He hoped the same thing would happen again, for his sake, this time.

It pained him to contemplate the alternative. If his father King did not receive his message, things looked bleak for him indeed. He was determined not to feel completely helpless. It was a feat that seemed nearly impossible. He couldn't even remember anything whatsoever of what had happened to him last night. This was unusual for him. Normally, he'd dream vivid dreams; occasionally even entering the mind of someone else and enjoying theirs as well. However, with his captors, he could not see anything beyond utter blackness even as they were seizing and transporting him from his comfortable bed chamber in the dead of night. This greatly distressed him, but he would have to deal with that unsettling issue later. For now, he had more pressing matters to attend to.

He surmised, judging by his enormous headache, that he must have been given something that made him vulnerable; otherwise, he wouldn't have ended up in this predicament. Normally, he would have known what they were up to from the start. He now realized with certainty that his special ability was not as perfect as he thought. There were limitations, despite what his father believed to the contrary.

As the sun rose in the sky, Oban glanced out from a small bolted window and saw birds flying overhead, only they were unlike any species he had ever known. Their wingspan was at least ten arms lengths, and their beaks were large enough to fit a human head within. Oban tried to be brave though the mere sight of them frightened him. As he steadied himself, he found himself oddly drawn to them somehow. They were eerily majestic. If not for his current circumstances, he might have enjoyed watching them soar through the sky—but not now. He desperately needed a plan to escape.

He looked further out, past the grounds and could see that he was in a very mountainous terrain. For a brief moment, it reminded him of his home, but unlike Degnal's mountains, these were creepily shaped with peaks that jetted out sharply like daggers. He was definitely no longer in his beautiful kingdom with its sweeping green rolling hills and the echoes of animals humming sweetly in the distance.

Suddenly, he could hear voices just outside the chamber door where he was currently jailed. Though he could not make out what they were saying, he concentrated and managed to read some of their thoughts. Whatever hampered him from doing so before was thankfully beginning to fade.

"'This cow piss should be perfect for the prince,' one of the men thought. While the other one had in mind, 'I don't like this business,' he thought, 'The boy scares me.' With that, the door abruptly swung open and in walked two foully clad servants. The larger one carried a bowl of something, while the other smaller one hovered in the doorway. The large one placed the bowl on a small table by the bed Oban was in, slamming it down and spilling most of its content onto the floor. Oban could smell the pungent aroma of urine splattering in every direction as the liquid made contact with the floor.

"Eat," said the larger one with a chuckle.

Oban nodded obediently all the while concentrating on his thoughts. Oban thought that the brute seemed far too comfortable in the presence of royalty. Though he did not concern himself with such formalities, he knew that his life was in danger around persons of this type. The larger man thought, 'I could do away with this one quickly and feed him to the wolves.' Then, without warning, he lunged at Oban.

Oban swiftly dodged the overgrown oaf by rolling off the bed and standing swiftly to his feet. The servant, now angry with his prey, lifted the bowl and flung it at Oban's head. Oban simply stepped aside as the vessel sailed past his eyes. With extended hands, the servant then leapt over the bed, arms stretched wide, hoping to wrap his fingers around Oban's neck. Oban timed his movement perfectly, allowing the man to be suspended in mid-air then only moving out of the way at the last possible moment. The servant landed face first onto the hard floor with a thump. Then, while the servant scrambled to regain consciousness, another man suddenly entered the chamber.

"You lazy fool! Get up!" the man shouted at the servant who was now struggling to rise to his feet.

While the servant was trying his level best to right himself, his little companion in the doorway, immediately rushed over and helped him up. Then, both quickly ran out, all the while glancing over their shoulder at Oban as they exited. Oban could hear their thoughts clearly, 'Devil,' he heard repeatedly. Oban nearly laughed aloud as they stumbled down the corridor.

"Prince, Oban," the new man said, greeting Oban somewhat cordially.

Oban did not think for a second that he was any better than the other two, though he did initially seem more gentile.

"Welcome to our modest land…" he said mockingly, "…I'm sure it pales in comparison to the great Degnal Kingdom…"

So far, Oban had managed to hear in his mind, between the man's words, where he was and why he was there. Only, he waited patiently for the man to tell him verbally as not to alarm him in any way. His father, King Degnal, had warned him against impatiently responding to others' thoughts rather than their speech. Unfortunately, the older he got, the harder it was for him to restrain himself.

"…I see that you haven't eaten your morning meal…" the man said, "…I will have another brought to you immediately. Would you like that?" he asked Oban who was reluctant to answer.

Oban nodded, yes, knowing it would be more of the same. For, to his dismay, the land he now found himself in was Treshville, a devastated part of the world considered the wasteland of the Great Lands. It was a kingdom without a king. Its resources long gone, picked clean by fierce storms or by roaming bandits taking anything of value and whisking it away. The few inhabitants who remained, experienced the turbulence of having one new ruler after another, each harsher than the last. Each brutal faction rose up killing off the previous regime. No one could be trusted within its borders.

The current, newly minted government was headed by a man named, Owitti. Oban would find out later that he became leader by lying, telling everyone he was an orphan. He did so to garner sympathy. It worked. He became one of the most popular of Treshville rulers by surrounding himself amongst men who took pleasure abducting rich people and making their families pay for their safe return.

Despite receiving silver, gold, and other valuables from desperate families, they had never kept their promise to return any loved ones. Instead, they each took turns killing their prisoners, solely for entertainment purposes. Their specialty was taking the person by surprise, betting on who could accomplish the task nasty first. Oban now knew that the two men from earlier had attempted to do just that, but fortunately for him, he was ready for them. He only hoped his good fortune could be sustained throughout this ordeal.

Oban felt certain that this new man before him did not wish to attack him, not yet anyway. Judging from his demeanor and conversation, Oban gathered that he was quite possibly the scholar amongst the other villains. Oban got the impression that he actually wanted to know more about Oban and especially about his kingdom, Degnal.

"You are far younger than any of our other…ah…guests…" he began humorously.

Oban raised his chin and then lowered it slowly, indicating that he understood. The mere fact of his young age may have played a factor in him not being murdered in his sleep. He wasn't naïve enough to suppose that it would remain a sufficient incentive. Oban had just turned fourteen winters at the last rounded moon.

"…and already destined for the throne?" he asked.

Again, Oban nodded, but did not speak. He had a nagging feeling from deep within not to engage in conversation with this man. There was something about him that Oban didn't like. Perhaps it was his droopy eyes, or his long, unkempt beard, that hung well past his neck and shoulders, and was so dirty and stiff, it never touched his chest. His skin draped his body like an ill-fitted wardrobe, brown and ashen, and what was left of his hair was splattered upon his oddly-shaped head in porous patches. Not to mention, there was something altogether off-putting about his face, possibly the two-to-three teeth that jetted out of his mouth when he spoke.

"…What, no words for a poor, old man, who would like to hear the exploits of a finer, richer class?" he asked much too proudly.

Oban started to correct him, then thought better of it and just lowered his head and hoped the old man would receive this gesture as a way of ending this idle chatter. After a good length of time, the old man continued to stand opposite Oban without moving.

Suddenly, the door flew open and in marched, Oban

surmised to be, Owitti, followed by no less than fifty men. Oban tried to steady himself, but the sight of them, took his very breath away.

"Anything?" Owitti asked the old man.

"Not a word, king…" the old man said, "…he just might be smarter than the rest."

"Smart, or not, we will kill him too," Owitti spat and grabbed Oban's shoulder and hurled him into the mob of men who followed him.

The men lifted Oban high above their heads, then threw him through the chamber entrance, down a corridor and eventually out into daylight. To his dismay, Oban was helpless to defend himself. He quickly discovered that he was no match for the massive throngs of men who, without much effort, now overpowered him. Worse off, the sun momentarily blinded him. He couldn't see anything. Plus, the thoughts he tried desperately to steal from anyone around seemed to rush at him en masse, making it nearly impossible for him to receive a clear train of thought.

Before he knew it, he was thrown into a body of rushing water. The current was so severe, it pushed him against a boulder, pinning him there for several moments while a heavy stream pounded his limbs. Suddenly, someone reached in and snatched him out. He went sailing down hard onto the earth that was filled with dirt, rocks and gravel. He felt as if he'd been pummeled. That's when someone ran towards him and kicked him squarely in his back. The pain was unbearable. He cried out in agony, but before he had time to adjust, someone else came forward and stomped on his hand, applying their full weight then stomping again and again, until his fingers began to break one by one.

As much as he did not wish to give them the satisfaction, tears began to stream down his face, especially as one by one the men approached and kicked, hit, and pulled at his increasingly broken body. He hadn't any way of defending himself from their torturous advances. He was just a child and even his special abilities seemed no match for a mob.

Then, with his life slowly ebbing away while they struck him repeatedly as he lay on the ground, he wondered where his father was and why he hadn't come to rescue him yet. He was sure he'd sent word. He now realized that his mental messages may not have been enough.

CHAPTER 5. King Runmari was still reeling over the recent demise of Degnal's Advisor, Burton; his would-be Degnal informant. Though he had never fully trusted the man, he greatly desired to use him as a means to gain the treasured Degnal Kingdom and add it to his growing list of prized territories. He found it clever of King Degnal to blame him for Advisor Burton's demise, a nice touch in King Degnal's deception. King Runmari had been planning to do the same, only in reverse. Once Advisor Burton's usefulness was at an end – he would be too, with King Degnal named as the cause of whatever mischief Runmari had in mind for the foolish old man. The late Advisor Burton represented King Runmari's second chance of seizing the Degnal Kingdom. It slipped from his grasp. Apparently, King Degnal had outwitted him again. King Runmari seethed for many days about that.

Fortunately, that morning, a new chance for him to take Degnal Kingdom emerged from a very unlikely source. King Runmari could hardly contain his excitement. Trained for battle since birth, he rarely showed emotion, but inside he was as giddy as a child. So much so, he was still savoring the delicious news he had received that night. He now knew something that even King Degnal was unaware. He was given the whereabouts of Degnal's one and only son, Prince Oban. One of Runmari's spies informed him over supper that the young Prince had been abducted in the middle of the night and was now being held captive in Treshville, of all places, by a rogue named Owitti.

Regrettably, King Runmari knew Owitti well. In fact, he had known him since his youth. He and Owitti were half-brothers. Their father, now deceased by assassination, had many wives and sired a multitude of children. So great a number, that at one point, King Runmari could scarcely keep count. With such a massive number of siblings, and with no father to govern them, they became estranged. Even while their father alive, they were never truly close, more like strangers—until King Runmari began his quest to rule the Great Lands.

Though ruthless and murderous himself, King Runmari was considered the stable brother amongst the others. Many of his conquered lands had one of his own family members posted there to oversee, govern but mostly to protect it. Even his aging mother operates one of his territories; one located by the ocean. She lives there to this day. This was why most of his family, though sizable, regarded him respectfully and feared him somewhat reverently. All save, Owitti.

Owitti had decided early on that he was going to be his own man. He rejected the lands that King Runmari conquered. He wanted to make a name for himself by doing some conquering of his own.

Unfortunately, many moons had passed since Owitti set out to achieve this goal, and all he had to show for it was a trail of disappointments. He was not built for battle, with his scrawny body, short stature and hunched shoulders. Therefore, he could not acquire territories by force like his burly, rugged, tall brother, King Runmari; with skin the color of black coal, and narrow piercing eyes that could intimidate most men with just a stare. Owitti also lacked the ability to oversee regions. He believed that diplomacy was for weaklings. So, at his hands, grounds were uncultivated, and inhabitants literally starved. Too selfish for his own good, he didn't believe in sharing the wealth. Since he lacked the knack or skill to achieve anything legitimately, the only thing he was truly suited for was utter destruction. For that, he was a master. It was no surprise to King Runmari that his loathsome brother, Owitti, would be the newly elected leader of Treshville, head of the cutthroats, ruffians and thieves. It's doubtful that anyone in his family would be proud of such an accomplishment, but King Runmari would feign approval nonetheless to appear cordial at their meeting.

As King Runmari ate his morning platter of wild goat and warm beer, he thought long and hard about how he was going to approach this current situation. With such a vast army, he had plenty of options at his disposal. The likes of a wasteland such as Treshville were no match for him. He could have easily taken the land many moons ago with minimal effort. In truth, it wasn't even a small challenge. Besides, the territory was practically barren. It had no natural resources left. Each conquering regime came and stripped the area clean of any worth it had ever had. Even its forests were emptied of most of their trees, used for lumber and kindling. The only inhabitants still residing there were either slaves, or people so poor they had no other choice than to serve the most recent ruling power.

Later that day, King Runmari, accompanied by no less than one hundred and fifty of his strongest armed guards peacefully rode into Treshville. King Runmari hoped his brother, Owitti was in good spirits, but in case he was not, he decided to be at the ready for anything. He brought thirty cases of his best beer in an effort to keep the conversation affable. He was only there to talk, possibly negotiate and nothing more. He even brought his cook along so that the entire visit would seem friendly and celebratory. Although, he'd dare say, that even the idea of sharing a meal with his brother did not appeal to him at all, but he'd make the best of it. However, if his brother denied him and wished to fight, King Runmari was, of course, armed to the teeth.

Immediately, upon King Runmari's arrival, he heard a commotion coming from the center of the abysmal place. It was so loud, the ruckus swelled out clamorously in every direction. King Runmari and his men could see dust and dirt liberally flying out from this crowd of the dirtiest, most foul-mouthed men they had the displeasure to come across in a long while. The crowd's purpose seemed like a simple reunion, but the overall mood was that of sport. A rousing choir of "Ayes!" rang out now and again, interspersed with laughter and boisterous cheers.

As he drew near, King Runmari could see that the entire den was converging upon some helpless sod. He couldn't even make out who it was because there were so many men upon their victim. King Runmari ordered his men to stand down, not wanting them to get mixed in with the den. Then he rode closer to where he saw his brother seated aloft.

Upon being eye to eye with Owitti, he greeted him as warmly as he could muster, though the pretense took considerable effort.

"Kill him, if you dare!" Owitti shouted to the unruly mob, ignoring his approaching guest with intention.

"Aye!" the crowd cheered.

Owitti then nodded his head toward King Runmari as if discovering him there at a distance. That was all Runmari would receive as a 'Hello.' He was well aware of this tactic. Owitti did not wish to appear frightened by the presence of such a large legion, at least not in front of his rag-tag forces, such as they were. King Runmari realized at that moment that he was going to have to witness the killing of the poor individual beneath the kicks and fists before he would have an uninterrupted audience with Owitti. Without hesitation, he turned his horse around, and despite the urgency of his quest, began watching Treshville's recreation.

Then, suddenly, a whooshing sound came from out of nowhere and rushed towards them. It appeared to be coming from the devastated forest off to the east. It grew louder as it rapidly approached, rising swiftly above the brawl. King Runmari glanced over at his guards and with a simple nod charged them to stay diligent. Unlike his wayward brother, who sat motionless, King Runmari was not going to be caught unawares. Meanwhile, the distant sound began to take on a shape as it now soared from out of the brush. To everyone's astonishment, it was the largest bird they'd ever seen. It was enormous, and it seemed to be precisely targeting the crowd where the fighting was taking place.

The horde didn't seem to notice it at first. Meanwhile, Owitti looked positively panic-stricken as the giant hawk-like bird swooped down and jammed his beak into the head of one of the men in the midst. The man stumbled to the ground, blood gushing down his face. Before any of the other men could react, the bird spun around and knocked three more men off their feet. Some nervously laughed, while others picked up rocks and sticks and began throwing them at the animal, but none managed to hit their mark. The hawk masterfully zoomed high in the air evading every strike.

King Runmari was in awe of the creature before him.

If he hadn't seen it with his own eyes, he wouldn't have believed it. He couldn't be certain, but it seemed to him as if the beast was fighting for the poor soul lying prostrate on the ground. 'Who could it be that fowl of the air would come to his rescue?' he pondered.

Meanwhile, Owitti stumbled from his perch in order to gain a closer look at the mayhem below while making completely sure he was far from it.

"Ah…" he uttered helplessly.

Then he turned slowly toward King Runmari with a scowl upon his face.

"I suppose this is your doing?" he asked.

King Runmari wasn't taken aback by the question. He was flattered. If only he could command animals in this way, he would surely be even more undefeatable. He merely turned to his hapless, half-brother and smiled, thinking he should take the credit whether he deserved it or not.

"Make it stop!" Owitti commanded him.

King Runmari laughed at the notion. Then he turned to see Owitti's band of misfits scampering to-and-fro as the giant bird began to swing its mighty wings at them. The force of the blows sent men flying high in the air. Some fell to the ground never to rise again. While others tried tirelessly to do battle with the mighty creature. Those the beast could not strike, it scratched with its long, sharp claws. With that, finally, the men began to retreat and as they did so, others launched arrows at it. The bird maneuvered swiftly out of reach by spinning up and ducking and dodging the weapons with ease. King Runmari thought, 'Impressive!'

"What evil magic is this?" Owitti asked, believing wholeheartedly that his estranged brother had come to seize his kingdom.

"I'm afraid, brother, this is none of my doing," King Runmari finally admitted.

Owitti did not take him at his word, but pouted at the idea that his conquering sibling was innocent of such a spectacular feat. King Runmari was thoroughly entertained by both the spectacle and the absurd notion that Owitti believed he had come to claim a land as loathsome as Treshville.

Then, as the cloud of dust began to settle over the melee, the hawk descended one last time into the midst and this time rose up carrying the bloodied victim gently within its talons. That is when King Runmari could see for the first time exactly who had been so helplessly at the mercy of Owitti and his men. Nothing could prepare him for what he saw. King Runmari turned sharply to Owitti.

"Are you mad?" he asked.

Owitti did not answer.

"Why kill the boy?" King Runmari asked, "…You could get a tremendous treasure for bringing him back alive to his homeland."

"We had no intention of killing the boy…" Owitti corrected his brother, "…We just wanted to teach him a lesson."

"And what lesson have you taught him?" King Runmari asked.

Owitti shrugged his shoulders and lowered his head. He did not feel that he needed a lecture on governing his kingdom, especially not from someone who hadn't bothered to be in his life for such a lengthy time.

"There is something strange about that one…" Owitti muttered, "…He's evil."

"Oh, so now, you do admit of wanting to kill the lad…to rid him of evil spirits, perhaps?" King Runmari laughed.

"See for yourself…" Owitti argued, "…That thing,

that bird came to save him!"

King Runmari looked off in the distance, still able to see the wings of the mighty hawk flapping, holding its load. It was none other than young Prince Oban.

CHAPTER 6.

"Come here," Queen Mother commanded.

Asha obeyed but not too quickly. She was a woman now and felt averse to bowing down to anyone let alone her now ancient mother. 'How dare she order me around as if she were still a useful Queen?' Asha thought, '…More like an old sack.'

"Let me look at you," Queen Mother requested. Then forcefully, she added, "In the light!"

Asha dragged her feet. She thought nothing of her royal duties anymore. As far as she was concerned, they were permanently in the past along with her mother.

She stood before what she considered the crowned fossil, shifting her weight from side to side; bored by this particular loathsome task. The Queen didn't seem to notice her daughter's bad behavior, but continued to take her time carefully scrutinizing her offspring. Asha decided to do the same right back to her. She narrowed her eyes and took a really good look at her Queen Mother. In her opinion, she did not look well. In fact, she realized at that moment something increasingly odd about her indeed. When suddenly the Queen turned Asha around and barked, "What means this?"

"What do you mean…?" Asha replied, and stopped short of mouthing, 'Old woman?'

"How many moons are you along?" Queen Mother asked bluntly.

Asha's face blanched, however; she did not convey her true feeling of alarmed rage. She thought, 'Of all the people to discover my secret.' She never would have believed it would be her absent-minded Queen Mother.

"You are mistaken, Queen Mother," Asha swiftly and softly spoke making sure to keep every contour of her face perfectly still.

"You believe me an old fool, don't you?" Queen Mother smirked.

Asha dearly wished to say yes, but realized that she had to play nice lest all be revealed before its due time. All plans would be lost if her Queen Mother told the King.

"Those words will never be on my lips, Queen Mother," Asha correctly told her.

Though she indeed thought them, she knew better than to say them out loud, for to offend the Queen Mother meant death.

"Wise choice, my daughter," Queen Mother said sternly, showing physical signs of fatigue at this point in the conversation.

Meanwhile, Asha stood rigidly, bracing herself for what was to come next.

"Who – is – he?" Queen Mother asked more as a command than a question.

Asha thought about it quickly and realized that she had but one choice - deniability.

"To whom are you referring to, Queen Mother?" Asha responded, deciding perceptively that her only way out of this inconvenience was to pretend she didn't understand.

Queen Mother lowered her head and breathed heavily.

"Leave us," Queen Mother whispered.

Asha turned on her heels and scurried towards the door, but just as she approached it, she heard her Queen Mother speak again.

"You weren't taken after all…" Queen Mother said, "...were you?"

Asha froze and listened.

"…You ran off as if you were a common servant…" Queen Mother continued, "…Mark my words…this will not end well for you or for him."

CHAPTER 7. Prince Oban awoke with a start, groggy and still reeling from his ordeal with the likes of Owitti and his cruel men. Yet, other than feeling a bit sore all over, it surprised him that he could still move about. A while earlier, that thought seemed impossible as he lay prostrate being practically pummeled to death. It was an utter miracle that he had escaped with his life. For that he was grateful, but how? Now what? Where was he? Who saved him?

This entire ordeal had left him completely out of sorts. While it was all taking place, he was certain that he had to have been dreaming. At one point he felt as if he were floating among the clouds, literally airborne high above tree tops and mountain peaks. It was so real that he yet held a picture of the aerial view in his mind. So vivid, he swore he smelt fresh rain, and could almost feel the heated sun upon his body. So real, he remembered his stomach churning with fear and exhilaration at the same time for the grand heights in which he swirled. With that thought, he lifted his head and craned it out to see exactly where he was lying.

Rocking too far forward, he suddenly panicked, for

all he saw was the sky. His heart thundered within his chest. Although frightened beyond measure, he gingerly eased himself over to get a better look, but unfortunately, before he knew it, he went sailing briskly downward, with nothing to stop his fall.

Suddenly, he couldn't breathe. His body went limp. He now found himself plummeting to the earth from an immense height. He flailed about wildly, desperately trying to clutch anything that would arrest his descent. Dreadfully, there wasn't anything to his right or left just open air. Then, out of nowhere, he heard a shrill cry coming from a great distance. It sounded like one of the many stray cats in Degnal Kingdom howling at the night sky. It didn't take long for him to realize that it was his own voice screaming for help. Fearing he was once again beyond hope, he was dismayed to hear only his own frantic screech. He couldn't believe that he had managed somehow to break free from violent villains only to now fall to his demise. What was happening? Why was he in this predicament? Regrettably, he hadn't the time to answer any of the hundreds of questions racing through his mind.

He only had but one that needed to be answered and it was to his father, King Degnal. 'Why have you not come?' he asked in deep sorrow as to why his very father hadn't bothered to rescue him. He longed for his homeland. Oh, how he missed it with its grass filled valleys as far as the eye could see. Everything about it seemed to echo in his heart. Tears moistened his face because he was quickly coming to grips with the idea of never seeing any of it again. He thought, in resolve, 'I will not see fifteen winters.' He would have enjoyed going on the quest of manhood. As a prince, he had been in training for it since birth. His tutors were preparing him for that very task. He learned all of the arts required, including hand-to-hand combat, the seven dialects of the Great Lands, survival techniques in the dark forest and at sea, as well as equestrian skills, and weaponry.

It pained him to discover that all of those many lessons were now a waste of time. He was filled with shame knowing that he had failed the test before it had even begun. For it was the Degnal tradition that any male child of that age who did not even show up for his contest, would be automatically disqualified and forced to live in exile. He thought it fitting that at least Degnal did not have to oust him from the Kingdom. He was already far, far away from home. 'I'll never return…' he thought, as he spiraled downward, '…How fitting to be snatched away by trickery, beaten to near death and now to sail into an abyss.'

Chinaza found a shady spot along-side an opening in the unruly brush. She saw a flat, smooth boulder and wearily sat down upon it to rest. She hadn't realized how tired she was until she did so. Her aching legs draped the stone and her back and shoulders drooped heavily downward. Her thoughts were about the past two moons. She couldn't believe how much had changed. In seconds her eyes moistened with sadness. She had lost everything. Nothing would ever be the same again. At the rising sun she had witnessed the Kenneth army slay all the men in her village. The images haunted her so that she had hardly slept since.

Unfortunately, with all the grief she felt for their deaths, she also was overwhelmed with a sense of shame. She couldn't believe that the mightiest men of her village didn't even fight back. She watched as they just stood there and allowed the opposing army to run them in. Chinaza was so incensed that she grabbed her father's ax, ran out of her hut, and charged the foreigners herself, only to be pulled back inside by her mother.

Afterwards, the incident filled her with such rage

that she ran out of the village in the middle of the night on, of all things, the family mule; the slowest beast they owned. Though she lied to her mother that she would warn the neighboring village, she hadn't decided any clear direction. Her only the desire was to flee in haste from what she surmised was the most severe bout of cowardice she'd ever seen. It was only by sheer coincidence that before she knew it, she was approaching the Kassel Village gates. It was Larson's neighboring village, but she hadn't intended to venture there. She was simply running away from her troubles.

The Kassel guards immediately welcomed her inside and when asked where she was from, she answered by telling them about the Kenneth army. Unlike her homeland, the Kassel guards got to work equipping themselves for battle and all the while thanking Chinaza profusely for her bravery. She knew better. She knew that she hadn't even given Kassel a second thought. However, she was glad that they would be saved even though her home had been viciously ruined.

Chinaza lifted her head from her sorrowful melancholy for the first time since all of her troubles began. Everything that had transpired from the moment she awoke seemed like a horrible nightmare. Reaching Kassel Village that dreadful night only magnified her uncertainty of the world she once knew. And that was especially compounded when Kassel villagers started thanking her profusely for thinking of them. Initially, it was so absurd to her that it nearly made her laugh in their faces. She knew that it was never her intention to alert Kassel Village. She was well aware that the thought never crossed her mind. In fact, she had only been to Kassel Village once. It was during the grand summer fair when her father went there to sell wool blankets. He insisted that the entire family join him. The memory of him nearly pulled Chinaza back into her grief. She hadn't any more tears to shed though because she suddenly realized hunger gnawed at her.

She reached in her satchel, the one given her by some of Kassel's welcoming mothers. To her surprise, tears filled her eyes again as she opened it to find sweet bread, the same as her mother made. Her first bite nearly made her faint with homesickness. She sat perfectly still until that wave of loneliness passed. She wished she could be as brave as the Kassel people believed her to be, but in reality, she was simply a scared little girl. She gently wiped the water from her eyes with the back of her hand and that is when she saw something that nearly took her breath away.

She was gifted with clear vision and knew that she was wide awake, but what she saw right in front of her seemed impossible nonetheless. From the very sky sailing at a dangerously quick pace was what appeared to be a boy.

Chinaza jumped from the rock and sprinted as fast as she could in his direction, dropping sweet bread along the way as she ran. She hurried quickly not knowing what she would do if anything to help the soul. She just knew that with a fall like that, he was going to need assistance. She feared she wouldn't reach him in time. She wondered where he might have come from. She didn't see any large trees or mountains from which he might have fallen. It didn't make sense. Where did he come from? Why was he flying through the air? Who was he? All these questions filled her mind as she tore through the thick fields, she hoped, to his rescue, but nothing could have prepared her for what she saw when she found him.

In a clearing, not very far from where she was originally seated, Chinaza saw him. There before her lay a boy. She didn't know what to expect, but she didn't think she'd find what she saw. To her surprise, even at a distance, he looked as if he was merely sleeping. She wasn't very knowledgeable of such, but knew enough to know that someone falling that fast, from that great of a height, should be severely wounded. However, this boy looked as if he didn't have a scratch on him. Chinaza once sled from a mule and had to remain abed the length of half a summer. With that in mind, she became even more suspicious of this boy as she approached.

She walked no further. 'What kind of dark magic is this?' she thought. She grabbed a stick from the tall grass and shaped it in her hands to swing at him. Gone were the thoughts of saving him. Now, if he steered, she might kill him.

But, before she knew it, curiosity got the better of her. She walked a bit closer to get a better look. Slowly, she ventured until she was almost standing over him. He didn't move at all when she approached. She used that time to observe him. 'Watch for breath,' her father would say about an animal they'd trap. Chinaza looked at the boy's stomach to see if it was raising and falling. It did. She scurried away in fear. 'He's alive,' she thought. Somehow that thought of him being alive scared her more than the thought of him being dead. She calmed herself and approached the prostate boy again.

As she did so, she could have sworn she heard a noise coming from the tall grass. Unfortunately, there could be any number of wild animals about and she momentarily berated herself for not being better prepared. She hadn't a single thing to protect herself save a stick. Normally, she'd have her knife, or her bag of stones, but foolishly she'd left those trusted weapons with the mule. 'The mule,' she thought, 'I left him to fend for himself as well.' She couldn't believe her many errors that day. She was usually more responsible. She looked down at the boy and thought, 'It's all your fault,' and raised the stick to strike him out of sheer anger.

With the tree branch above her head, she saw out of her periphery the largest beast she'd ever seen in her life. Then, with the stick still raised overhead, she watched in horror as it charged right toward her as if to strike her down.

"Ahhhhh!" she shrieked.

"No," someone whispered.

And with that small voice, barely an audible sound, the creature stopped short, turned its enormous head and sat obediently down in the tall grass. Chinaza was stunned. She stood frozen, mouth agape, struggling for her own voice, and just looked upon the thing awestruck. At second glance, it appeared as if the animal was now sunbathing. It was completely uninterested in her now and seemed as if it didn't have a care in the world. Mere moments ago, Chinaza feared for her life being utterly at the mercy of such a brute. Now, it looked like one of her stray dogs seated calmly awaiting supper. She didn't even notice the boy who was now standing right beside her.

"Aye!" she exclaimed, startled by his sudden appearance nearby.

"Oh, sorry…" Oban said, "...I didn't mean to frighten you."

"I wasn't frightened," Chinaza said indignantly, tossing away the stick that she realized was still clasped between her fingers.

"I see," Oban mouthed and backed away a bit.

He didn't have to steal her thoughts to see that she didn't like their proximity.

"I'm Oban," he said in greeting.

Chinaza merely glared at him.

"And, you are?" he asked.

"Chin…Chin…" she trailed off.

"Chin?" he asked for clarity.

"Why do you want to know?" she snapped.

"Well, I'm just curious…" he pondered, "...We don't know each other...We're alone in this area...and…"

"And, what?" Chinaza barked, "...Why do you say we're alone and… Do you mean to have that thing attack me?"

"No!" Oban said, "No."

Chinaza didn't completely believe him and stole a look at the animal. It was now resting peacefully. No longer the towering menace. It almost, of all the frightening things, looked gentle.

"I just wanted to ask a question and thought if I knew your name, I'd know to whom I was addressing," Oban tried.

"Chinaza," Chinaza reluctantly muttered.

"Chinaza…" Oban smiled, "...It's nice to meet you."

Chinaza didn't smile back, but lowered her eyes on Oban cautiously. She had no desire to be entangled with the likes of him, this boy. She worried that she may have made a mistake coming to his rescue in the first place. 'Not a scratch on him,' she thought.

"What are you anyway?" Chinaza asked, "...Part spirit? Part god? What?"

"Me?" Oban laughed, "No... No. Why do you ask me that?"

"You came from the sky," Chinaza told him matter-of-factly, as if he was unaware of that fact himself.

Oban stepped back and pondered what he must have looked like falling as he had. He was now greatly curious to know if she saw what occurred next. He hoped not. For as he plummeted to his certain death, the giant hawk sailed swiftly to him and cushioned itself beneath Oban to create a soft, and perfect landing. Oban never felt the ground beneath him; upon touching down, he was surrounded by feathers, and gently rolled to the grass. Yes, he hoped Chinaza hadn't witnessed any of that. She would definitely believe him a god. He might think himself one too, were it not for the fact that he knew otherwise. As prince of Degnal, he realized swiftly that he couldn't tell her that part of himself either. Being a prince in these foreign lands was not conducive to his health.

He raised his head and found Chinaza staring at him. He suddenly felt as if she knew his every thought. He didn't wish to reveal too much more. He had to tell her something. He needed her help.

"I'm just a boy from Degnal and I need to get home.

Can you help me?" he simply asked.

CHAPTER 8. Just before dawn, the Kenneth soldiers, thirsty for blood, looked ahead and could finally see Degnal's opulent palace in the distance. They were weary beyond reason, but having been outsmarted by every Degnal village they encountered other than Larson, they trotted fiercely onward straight towards the main gates.

The poison of Priest Godlumthakathi's spell still dripped from their weapons, but had now transformed itself from the smell of fresh war, to a kind of infection. It led the troops into a wicked, frenzied madness. They were dangerous now, not just to their enemies but also to themselves. Senseless fights broke out. From merely scrapping, scratching, and brushing up against their weapons, leaving some dead or dying. Random, inconsequential spats broke out as well, leaving their ranks drained of spirit. Unfortunately, it was in this same sorry condition that they approached Degnal palace.

The Kenneth Lieutenant, Talib, cried out to his men, "Ready?"

"Aye!" they roared back.

With that shout, the army charged down the field. Their spears, axes, and mallets in hand. They raced forward on their steeds determined to do away with Degnal once and for all. The sound of them battering towards the castle was like thunder, a great clamoring rumble designed to strike fear in the hearts of Degnal's soldiers.

To the Kenneth soldier's delight, at their charge, the great gate burst open and gave way with ease. The army rode through triumphantly. During this entire, abysmal war campaign, victory was finally at hand. Kenneth could almost reach out and touch Degnal's defeat now within their grasp. It was their good fortune. 'Degnal's King was careless,' they thought. And when they began to notice that no one had been roused, they began to shout wildly.

"Burn it down!" Talib roared.

But, before his soldiers began torching everything in sight, arrows, that were not their own, began flying towards them from outside the Degnal walls. These weapons were coming from the direction whence they came directly striking the Kenneth soldiers. Several soldiers fell from their horses, wounded deeply and bleeding. Others charged forward recklessly, looking in every direction for the culprits, while others retreated back quickly toward the entrance. Alas, as they raced back to the gate, the giant door began to close locking them in.

"It's a trap!" they shouted too late before the large wooden contraption shut leaving them inside Degnal's courtyard.

"Take cover!" Lieutenant Talib ordered his men.

With that, the Kenneth soldiers scurried in every direction, each looking for a means of shelter. Some actually did manage to squeeze out of the gate and thereupon ran for their lives, but the majority of the soldiers were now inside the walls exposed to a barrage of arrows sailing down upon their heads. Quickly, the ground beneath became soaked with blood as one soldier after another fell to his death.

Unbeknownst to the Kenneth army, King Degnal had been in a meeting with his most trusted servant, Commander Testlar, the night before they attacked.

"And yet they still have the nerve to wish to see me dead?" King Degnal asked Commander Testlar, with indignation.

Commander Testlar had told him of the villages who had defeated this army without lifting a single armament.

"How dare they!" shouted and King, "...And for what purpose? We haven't done anything, but take a few weapons, and for that they wage a war!"

"I heard from one of my most trusted spies that the Kassel visitors returned to Kenneth maimed.

"Maimed?" asked King Degnal.

"Yes, my King…" Commander Testlar told him, "...Each was missing his eyes and tongue."

"Surely they don't believe that any of my citizens had done such a thing," King Degnal contemplated.

It wasn't a question necessarily. Both already knew the answer. King Degnal would have preferred an audience with the Kenneth Elders to further discuss the matter. He had done trade with them many times and had always regarded them as allies. He had no desire to do battle with their army and especially not for a crime he hadn't even committed.

"Commander…" King Degnal began.

"Yes, my King," replied Commander Testlar.

"Dispatch some men immediately to the Kenneth territory…" King Degnal ordered, "...I will give them a message to relay before the Elders."

"I will ready the men straight away, my King," Commander Testlar replied, "And what of the approaching forces, my King?"

The King sat and thought gravely about his next move. As so often with being King, he wished that things were different. He knew all too well that all of his choices came with consequences that were froth with complications. Unfortunately, he could put his entire Kingdom in danger with one unwise decision.

"We will have to kill many of them, I'm afraid…" said King Degnal solemnly, "...You say one of our villages was destroyed without a single weapon being drawn, correct?"

"Yes, my King," Commander Testlar agreed.

"And able men stood still while they ran them in, right?" King Degnal asked.

"We received the same story from a host of witnesses, my King," Commander Testlar.

"The Kenneth army is not that strong as to overpower our great forces," King Degnal said mulling over this matter.

"No, they are not, my King…" Commander Testlar agreed, "…None of the Kennethians have even seen war up close."

"This must be the work of very dark magic…" King Degnal reasoned, "…How else does an entire village of men stand frozen and simply take that kind of torment?"

"How, indeed, my King?" Commander Testlar asked.

"We cannot consort with the likes of any of them at all, less we succumb to those same forces too," King Degnal said.

"You are a wise and mighty King," Commander Testlar told him.

They both knew that whatever transfixed their villagers could quite possibly bewitch them as well.

"We cannot risk it. We must dispatch them all I'm afraid…" King Degnal said, "…and quickly too."

Neither King Degnal nor Commander Testlar wished to do away with Kenneth's army. In fact, they believed them to be some of the bravest men in the Great Lands. Truly they did not have any issue with them either. In fact, Kenneth would frequent their villages considering Degnal a home away from home, and definitely an escape from their harsh winters. King Degnal knew their Elders and had consulted with them on many occasions in matters of diplomacy.

In King Degnal's mind, the Kenneth army had brought this great burden on themselves. They had angrily swept across the Degnal Kingdom without so much as an advance letter dispatched describing their grievances. What else could King Degnal do? The Kenneth army had employed the deadliest of dark arts. How else could they have made statues of his kingdom men? He had to protect his territory. It was out of his hands. He had to kill them all.

CHAPTER 9. Badu had decided many moons ago not to make himself party to any the festivities that might take place on this particular day. He was reasonably certain that given he was the tenth child of twenty he would not be missed. He figured everyone would gather together in celebration and not even give thought to the honored guest - him. For this was the day of the anniversary of his birth. He couldn't recall the exact day that he had stopped looking forward to it. Regretfully, it may have been as early as his fifth winter.

As he turned his back and walked far away from his village, he told himself that he hadn't any real interest in the assorted sweetened bread that would be served. Though the tantalizing aroma of his mother's baking almost made him retreat and surrender his protest. 'Was it too much to ask for pudding?' he muttered, knowing full well that his family, in fact his entire tribe, was too poor for such a tasty treat. Unfortunately, even if they were rich, there probably wouldn't be enough goodies to go around, he thought, and certainly none would be left for him. He looked down at his swollen belly rebuking his accursed rotund size all the while. Lately, his increasing girth had become a continued taunt throughout the village, especially from those within his own family.

"You're even bigger than your brothers!" his father exclaimed to him that very day.

It was the word 'even' that made him ever more distressed. As his father spoke, Badu held his breath to stop the tears from welling up in his eyes. He refused to be the cry-baby of the family, especially when there were actual babies in his family. Could he help the fact that he loved his mother's lamb stew so much? It wasn't his fault that her yams and dried fish were so delectable that he licked the edges of the table for crumbs. 'I can't help it,' he thought, somewhat angry with himself for not being able to stop himself from eating so much, as his thinner siblings routinely could, for even after he finished his portion, he sought to devour theirs as well. He couldn't understand how they could leave a single morsel.

He knew his father loved him, at least he wanted to believe that somewhere deep down there was a proud, broad smile reserved just for him. He envisioned a secret place shared by only he and his father, where there was a pat on the back followed by a "Good job, son." Within this dream world, Badu thought that he wouldn't be yelled at for simply being himself.

Unfortunately, Badu's family could not be categorized by anyone who knew them as a very affectionate one. In fact, Badu could scarcely recall a single time when his father, or mother for that matter, had ever wrapped their arms around him and pulled him close. He saw other families do such things, but not his. What did he expect? His father was a hunter by trade. Therefore, all of their lives were focused around trapping animals, slaughtering them and selling their meat and fur. This was tough employment and not for the faint at heart; one where only the brave and fearless of the tribe took part. In Badu's family, very little else was spoken of in their small, but clean well-organized hut. It was after all the family business. Even his mother and sisters spent the majority of their time preparing food, clothing, and moral support so that his father and older brothers would be ready for their hunts. Alas, Badu was never included in any of these activities; neither helping with preparations, nor going into the wild with his father and brothers. His father told him once that he would just get in the way.

"We don't want to mistake you for a bear!" his father said to him once with a smirk.

Badu was deeply wounded by that statement. He could think of nothing else as he walked away from everything resembling the familiar. The only thought on his mind was to put as much distance between he and his family as possible.

There he was that afternoon in an open field trudging along with his head and spirits bowed low. Ironically, it was one of the few places that might be considered private. He was grateful. He could finally cry without the world watching. And he allowed the tears to flow, and flow they did. Regrettably, by the time the pain in his heart started to subside, he realized rather abruptly that he was lost.

He panicked as he quickly glanced back and couldn't see anything recognizable, especially with the now setting sun. All he saw were shadows and dark patches looming creepily upon the path he just trod. He was suddenly shaken. In strict abeyance of his father's wishes he had never ventured beyond the hunting grounds before. He didn't understand why there was such caution given to him for merely roaming around until now. This area looked like a wasteland to him, equipped with spooky clusters of oddly shaped trees amidst a jagged, rocky landscape. It didn't take him long to grasp that he was utterly off course. All at once, that thought compounded his anxiousness. The feeling was so intense that eventually he became weary. Now tired and overwhelmed, he decided the best thing for him to do was rest. If he had any hope of returning home, he needed at least a modicum of energy to think. He found an enlarged boulder and plopped down telling himself that once he regained his strength, he'd get back his bearing.

Meanwhile, in another open field, there was Oban and Chinaza still locked in conversation. Chinaza took a few moments to mull over her situation. She didn't wish to return home and be reminded of the loss of her father and brothers. And, she hadn't anywhere else to go. So, against her better judgment, she finally agreed to help Oban. It was her sheer sense of duty that ultimately won her over and nothing whatsoever to do with the likes of the scraggly, filthy boy before her. Simply put, he was benefiting from her parents' good breeding. Chinaza's survivalist knowhow was entirely to Oban's advantage. He had no idea that she knew these parts as well as any courier or tracker. This was where she was born and raised. She was fully acquainted with every lake, stream, meadow, mountain, tree and patch of earth. Her brothers took her along with them on practically all of their adventures and there she learned to fish, hunt and endure the wild as well as any male child. That's why she was able to escape Larson, her home, so masterfully.

Also, like her brothers, she didn't scare easily. That is why, even though she knew that Oban was not who he claimed, she would continue to converse with him until his true identity was made known. 'Anyone who could command a giant beast as he had could not be of this world,' Chinaza thought. In her mind she was in the presence of a god, a small, foul smelling one, but nevertheless, something supernatural. If her assumption was correct, she knew she had to assist him. If for no other reason, she didn't wish to not assist a deity. If, however, she was with a demon, she'd be ready for that too. On her mule was a long, sharp blade. She had killed animals with it for food. She didn't think it would be that difficult to do the same with Oban if that time arose. When she had a moment, she'd fetch it and place it in the fold of her dress.

Oban was truly thankful of their arrangement. Chinaza even allowed him to seat on the mule most of their journey. He had never been anywhere outside of Degnal's castle territory before. And as night fell, he was pleased to see that they had covered so much ground. He wasn't even tired. He felt sure that he could continue on and was confused when Chinaza informed him, "We have to find shelter now."

"You don't have to stop on my account. I can make it," Oban assured her that he had strength enough left.

"It's not you I'm worried about…" Chinaza said, "...It's the night creatures that eat anything that moves; who can see far better than we can in the dark."

It never occurred to Oban that he could be considered a meal. The thought was very unsettling.

"Yes...Yes...You are right…" Oban told her, "...Let's do that. You are wise."

A few arms lengths away from them there was a brae. Chinaza walked over to it and with a stick began digging into its surface. When Oban realized what she was doing, he picked up a twig and proceeded to help. Before they knew it, they had dug a hole adequate for the two of them to slip inside the crevice. It gave them just enough covering without feeling cramped.

"You're very clever," Oban said to Chinaza.

Chinaza didn't know how to take his compliment. She was only prepared to stab him if need be but not to thank him for being kind. She looked in every direction but his until he finally turned away.

"We'll need to leave the mule out unfortunately," Chinaza told him.

Oban listened to her thoughts. 'He'll have to walk now,' she thought. Once again, that was something Oban never really had to do - walk. He decided to settle into the slope of their little makeshift cave and try to get comfortable. Meanwhile, Chinaza left for a moment and came back with fallen branches. She used them to fortify the entrance. Oban reached out to assist only then to grasp the notion that he hadn't the way withal to do so. Chinaza reached in her sleeve, brought out some red sand and scooped out some to Oban.

"What's this?" he asked.

"Supper," Chinaza replied.

Oban understood much too late that the reaction upon his face wasn't anything resembling gratitude.

"I'll take it back then!" Chinaza snapped.

"No... No…" Oban said, "...I'll eat it. I'll eat it."

Chinaza reluctantly retreated.

"It's just that I never had this before," Oban confessed.

"You must live a charmed life then," Chinaza smirked.

Oban gave her a gentle smile all the while lamenting the life he had once lived. He hoped beyond measure that he could one day have it again, but after all that had transpired, he didn't think it possible. It was only then in their increasingly darkened shelter that he thought again of his father, King Degnal. 'Why has he not searched for me?' he thought. Of course, he didn't know where he was but surely someone would have been sent to seek out his whereabouts. By now he had placed many thoughts in his father's mind, thoughts of his surroundings and requests for him to come to his rescue. Alas, there was no answer, no soldiers roaming the countryside, at least none Oban had seen.

"How far are we from Degnal castle?" Oban asked Chinaza.

"Two days' walk, maybe three, I believe," Chinaza replied with a yawn.

Oban tried to muster a smile.

"I thought you'd be happy about that," Chinaza said.

Oban contemplated Chinaza's statement. In truth, the closer they got the more apprehensive he felt about returning. Was it still going to feel like home to him after all this time? And what of his father, the King? Did he still regard him as a son, or was he somehow replaced? What conclusion could Oban draw other than him being abandoned? The man he trusted above all others had decided that he no longer wanted him. Oban regretted the accursed day he was born.

With that, he rolled over and tried not to ponder his troubles any longer, though the thoughts persisted. He couldn't help but recall his father tracing all over from territory to territory in search of his only daughter, his sister, Asha. Oban had entered his mind one night and told him to immediately return home. That was when Degnal Kingdom was under attack by King Runmari.

Yet now, in his time of need, there wasn't a single scout searching the Great Lands on his behalf. In fact, it was as if he didn't even exist. Suddenly, he felt teary-eyed as he tried once more to send word to his father, King Degnal. He silenced all other thoughts to the contrary this time, squelching any doubt and concentrating only on his father. 'Father,' he thought, '...I'm in a wooded area now not very far from home.' To his utter surprise, he began to sense a connection between them. It was as warm as he had remembered but before he could share another thought...nothing. The invisible link was broken. There wasn't even a stir of a message coming back to him. It was as if his father dismissed the thought out of hand. If he would allow himself complete truth, that was the part that pained him. 'How can you not hear me?' Oban's thoughts cried. Then he turned his head away from Chinaza and sobbed in silence.

CHAPTER 10. After a fitful sleep, Oban awoke to find Chinaza standing over him with her hand tightly covering his mouth. Quickly, he read her thoughts, which said, 'Don't move.' Thankfully, she also gestured for him to remain silent and only when he was settled, gently lowered her hand and pointed outside of their hiding place. Oban braced for a wild animal, but to his surprise, a boy no older than him sat casually on a boulder. Oban looked over at Chinaza and they both shrugged their shoulders acknowledging the oddity of this situation.

"Should we say something to him?" Oban mouthed in hushed tones.

"No!" Chinaza whispered back emphatically.

She was loath to be with Oban let alone another stranger. Besides, she believed this new one would be an imperfect distraction.

"Although…" she said, "...a boar would go for that round one first before coming after us," she advised Oban.

Even though that would benefit them, Oban really didn't like the sound of it. It wasn't in his nature to just sit by and watch someone die on his account. His sense of duty would not allow it. So, without conferring with Chinaza first, he rushed out into the open to warn the stranger.

"Hello," Oban said.

Upon seeing Oban, the boy slid off the rock with a start. Meanwhile, Chinaza ducked out of sight.

"Ahhh!" he exclaimed, turning toward Oban, "I didn't see you there. You scared me."

"Apologies," Oban said, "...I didn't mean to. I'm Oban. What's your name?"

"I'm Badu," Badu said, "Nice to meet you. I didn't think I'd run into anyone else out here."

At that, Chinaza finally came out of the cave and eyed to two boys disapprovingly. She wasn't in the mood to be cordial and felt certain this new boy would assuredly get them all killed. By the looks of him she knew he wasn't good for much besides eating all their rations.

"Oh, that's Chinaza," Oban said nodding in her direction.

"Nice to meet you too, Chinaza," Badu said very much too cheerfully.

Chinaza frowned in Badu's direction and backed as far away from him as possible. Then she checked around the trees for the mule. There was no sign of it.

"Great!" she exclaimed, "The mule is gone," she

looked again to and fro, then in anger, "Can we go now?" she asked Oban without waiting for a response.

Briskly, she walked away from both boys. Oban followed, and without hesitation, so did Badu.

"Where do you think you're going?" Chinaza asked Badu.

"I'm…I'm…well…" Badu stuttered.

"'I'm well I'm…'" Chinaza teased.

"Are you lost?" Oban asked, glancing at Badu.

"Look at him…" Chinaza said with a smirk, "Of course he's lost."

"Well…I'm…I…" Badu uttered.

"Praise be to the gods," Chinaza sighed, "He'll only slow us down."

At Chinaza's harsh words, Badu stopped walking with them and instead began to retreat. Oban reached over, grabbed his arm and pulled him forward.

"Don't listen to her," Oban told him, "She knows the way to Degnal. That's where we're heading."

Badu's face brightened, "My family goes there to trade. If I go along with you maybe I'll meet up with them," Badu told Oban.

"See, you're not lost anymore," Oban said.

"I guess I'm not!" Badu replied.

Chinaza rolled her eyes skyward and kept walking swiftly with Oban and Badu trailing not far behind. Whatever the distance, they were too close for her liking. She would have preferred to be alone in these fields rather than hearing the inane chatter between what she considered to be the round one and the not to be trusted one.

"It is the anniversary of my birth today," Badu told Oban.

"Cheers, my new friend! Cheers!" Oban shouted, raising his voice for emphasis.

Chinaza stiffened and increased her pace, widening the distance between her and the boys.

"My village is celebrating it," Badu said.

"Without you?" Oban teased, "The honored guess."

"Who?" Badu asked.

"Why…you, of course," Oban explained.

"Me." Badu laughed, "...Yes…of course…me."

He then lowered his head in attempt at hiding the sorrowful look upon his face.

"How many winters are you? Oban asked.

"Fourteen," Badu said proudly.

"As am I," Oban told him.

“Can we go now?” Chinaza murmured over her shoulder as she walked even more quickly through the brush.

Oban and Badu happily followed.

Before long, nighttime began to fall on the three. They were weary and hadn’t eaten anything the whole way at the insistence of Chinaza. She didn’t wish to lose a moment of daylight especially since their new friend was indeed delaying their travels.

‘What I wouldn’t give to be back home at the feast right now,’ Badu thought, ‘Roast duck and dumpling, mince pie…perhaps even a bit of beer…’

‘That sounds delicious,’ Oban thought in response to Badu’s thoughts.

‘My father would have to hand me a mug of it because like he’s said…’ Badu thought then suddenly paused for a moment.

“Wait a moment...” Badu stopped short in his tracks, and said “…I have not heard your voice, nor mine…and yet…and yet…”

Oban froze. He was so worn out from their travels; he hadn’t realized that he had let his guard down. This was the one thing his father warned him of, responding to others' thoughts and not their words.

"And what?" Chinaza asked Badu suspiciously.

"And…and…and…he…well…" Badu stammered.

"He…he what?" Chinaza asked sharply.

"He answered me!" Badu exclaimed, "He answered me with his thoughts! I clearly heard him too and yet he had not said a word."

All three halted and eyed one another in complete silent. Unfortunately for Oban, the recognition of what had just occurred was not lost on any of them. Chinaza, in particular, remained still in heavy contemplation allowing Badu's words to sink in. Then she and Badu, none too subtly, backed as far away as possible from Oban.

"I knew it! I knew it!" Chinaza shrieked.

Before anyone could say a word, Chinaza took off through the brush fleeing with all her might from both boys. In her mind they both were bewitched. Oban and Badu quickly ran after her. Though, neither could really keep up. Chinaza's legs were strong. She leapt like a gazelle over the untamed land with ease, while Oban and Badu stumbled, and got tangled up in branches and leaves.

"She's too fast!" Badu cried.

"Chinaza! Please! I can explain!" Oban yelled, "I can explain," he tried, "Please wait!

After a lengthy while and a now considerable distance, Chinaza looked back and didn't see either one of them behind her. 'The gods are on my side,' she thought, 'I've outrun the evil one and his friend. I'm free.' She was greatly delighted, but that mood would not last. For she hadn't any place to go. Alas, she didn't have a home anymore, not without her father anyway. He meant everything to her and now he is was gone. All at once, the weight of her circumstance came crashing down upon her. She could feel the tears welling up in her eyes but before allowing herself the luxury of crying, she'd run some more perhaps to escape all of her misfortune if possible. She'd allow all the anger and pain she felt to dissipate in the breeze.

Unfortunately, as she turned to run again, she abruptly bumped into something or someone. The force of the impact knocked the wind out of her and she went sailing to the earth. Then there came a deep male voice that awoke her as if from a dream, "Pick her up!" At once, Chinaza was hoisted to her feet with the help of a rather large hand wrapped around her tiny wrist.

"Where are you going in such a hurry, girl?" asked the voice of the tallest, broadest, blackest man Chinaza ever laid eyes upon.

He was a menacing sight indeed, and the sound of him was intimidating. The imposing look of him was even worse. He was so huge that his enormous body blocked out the sun.

"Let me go!" Chinaza shouted.

"No one is holding you," chuckled the giant man.

At that, Chinaza turned to see that she indeed wasn't being held. Immediately, she seized that opportunity to flee, only to quickly realize that she was, however, being blocked by an entire army. To her dismay, she was surrounded by them.

"Don't touch me!" Chinaza warned while determining the best way to pull her blade from its sheath.

She knew she couldn't best a whole army, but she was determined to fight her way from them with her last breath if necessary.

"What's your hurry?" the man repeated, "Is there someone chasing you?"

Chinaza didn't wish to tell these foreigners anything.

She'd had her fill with the likes of people she didn't know. Besides, she could tell that lot weren't exactly interested in assisting her.

"No," she responded much too curtly.

"Aye, but your face says, yes," the man said to her rather perceptively.

Chinaza disliked him even more for his cleverness.

Then suddenly, in the distance, they all heard, "Chinaza, where are you? Chinaza!"

"Chinaza?" the tall man asked her confirming that that was her name.

Chinaza did not reply, but rather hoped that Badu would stop trying to find her.

"…You can come out now! He's not the son of Cimeries! Honest," Badu shouted.

After that, Badu shouted Chinaza's name again. Then he came out into the open to find Chinaza standing in the midst of a great hoard of soldiers. He felt exposed. Coming from his small village, he had never seen anything like it. They were fearsome with their metal armor, spears and axes. Even their mighty steeds snorted boldly in his direction as he stood now shaking in their presence. He wasn't quick enough to retreat but tried anyway, only to be blocked by men carrying weapons. He wished he hadn't jumped out so quickly, thinking if only he had seen them first. Unfortunately, everything was hidden from his view from behind the trees.

"What do we have here?" said the tall man who was obviously the leader in charge of this brood.

"I don't want him to come near me!" Chinaza screamed in panic, "Get him away from me!"

Badu didn't answer Chinaza because suddenly the army's weapons were pointing directly at him.

"Chinaza, it isn't me…" Badu tried, "...I haven't done anything..."

The more Badu spoke the closer to him the soldiers advanced.

"...Chinaza, don't…" Badu cried, "...Please…please...Make them…"

"Stop!" yelled a voice from beyond the trees.

Thankfully, for Badu, everyone turned in the direction of the interruption, including the armed men approaching him. Then slowly out walked Oban from the trees and into the field.

"King Runmari, it's good to see you again," Oban

said, formally addressing the exceedingly tall man standing prominently before them.

"Prince Oban…" King Runmari grinned, "...I'm glad to see that you are well…"

King Runmari was more than glad, he was overjoyed. He would now have yet another opportunity to obtain Degnal Kingdom by escorting their no longer missing future king to its front gate.

Chinaza and Badu tried not to over react at hearing the title, 'Prince!' Instead, they glanced at one another in recognition with a slight nod.

"...Last I saw you - you were being flown through the heavens by way of a dragon!" King Runmari chuckled.

Chinaza reflected on the first time she set eyes on Oban thinking she was dreaming only to have this 'King' confirm that what she thought she saw was real.

"Hardly a dragon…" Oban half-heartedly said correcting him, then adding, "...Just an unusually large bird."

Silence blanketed the assembly as everyone present stared wide-eyed, with mouths agape at both Oban and King Runmari.

"Come, come, Prince Oban…" King Runmari smiled, "...you are too modest about things that are unusually spectacular. Are you not?"

King Runmari's question sounded more like a challenge. Oban heard him thinking, 'He's just a boy, but there is dark magic at work.' Oban did not wish to deal with King Runmari in any way, shape or form, especially in light of his current situation with Chinaza and Badu. He was afraid he might get them all killed at the hands of, what he knew to be, a ruthless villain.

"Why, what do you mean, King Runmari?" Oban asked coyly, "I am just a lad making his way back home after being taken away against my will."

"Yes, yes, about that…" King Runmari began, "...Is it not unlike your father to not tear apart the countryside in search of his one and only son?"

The way he said 'only' made the hairs on the back of everyone's neck stand straight up especially Chinaza's. She didn't wish to die this way at the hands of a madman. With that thought in mind, she heard for the first-time what Badu experienced. She nearly flinched and gave it away, nearly, but she now heard Oban's voice clearly in her head. It was as if they were speaking face to face. 'Be still, Chinaza,' Oban told her in thought, 'He's trying to find a weakness.'

Chinaza held her breath in order to stop herself from

shaking, not from fear but from anger. At that precise moment, a plan began to develop in her mind. She couldn't believe how extraordinarily focused she began under this much pressure. Her senses became heightened and her vision sharp. She knew exactly what they had to do. 'Tell him we're hungry,' Chinaza told Oban in thought. She quickly got used to Oban's oddity, but she still did not completely trust him. She was no longer hesitant to use his magic. However, it did startle her when Oban immediately obeyed her request.

"King Runmari, we've been walking for days, and…" Oban said.

Before Oban could finish his sentence, King Runmari waved to one of his servants. The servant quickly ducked into a nearby hut and returned just as fast with a large tray of food. Oban and Chinaza raced over to it before Badu, to everyone's surprise. Badu was still winded from their run and overheated from the sun. Once he got his bearing again though, he joined Oban and Chinaza.

King Runmari watched the three intently as they devoured their meal. They did so in absolute silence. It was the quietness that made him take note of their behavior. Little did he know, but they were talking to one another through the power of thought. Chinaza thought, ‘When I was a child my brothers and I used to float under the water using reeds.’ Oban replied in thought, ‘Like those over there?’ Oban nonchalantly nodded to some fallen branches from a large bamboo tree.

When Oban placed that thought into Badu’s mind, Badu rolled his eyes around in a circle before looking at the pile. He frowned, and shook his head indicating, ‘No.’ He was a bit less enthusiastic than Chinaza and Oban. In fact, upon hearing the full details, he immediately thought that the plan wouldn’t work. Hearing Badu’s thoughts, Oban reassured him that it would. Then he made it clear that they didn’t have many options. He also warned him sternly that they were among men who thought nothing of killing for sport. After hearing Oban’s words, Badu quickly warmed up to the idea of at least giving the plan a try.

Meanwhile, King Runmari continued watching the three with their frantic head nods and random eye moments. Everything about them made him trust them less and less, though their movements seemed humorous to him at the same time. He assumed that their near starvation had produced a kind of delirium. Eventually, he grew weary of the three, and walked back to rejoin his army. He had a plan of his own that he wanted his men to perform. Once he reached the other side of the camp, King Runmari advised two of his most ruthless men to keep Oban and get rid of the rest by early light. As far as he was concerned, Oban was the only one worth keeping.

As soon as King Runmari turned from the three, Chinaza gestured to the guard King Runmari left with them that she needed to relieve herself. To Chinaza's delight, the guard tilted his head towards the trees. She couldn't believe her eyes because the guard was pointing to the Bamboo. It took her seconds to sweep three reeds beneath her skirt and tuck them under her sash. Moments later, she was back on the ground seated with Oban and Badu. Badu marveled at Chinaza's cleverness of holding three pieces of wood completely hidden from sight. Badu didn't have to read Chinaza's mind to know that she was none too pleased with the toothy grin he was giving her. Badu was no fool. He lowered his head straightaway and continued gnawing the terribly tough mutton and stale bread.

'Now what?' Badu thought. Oban placed a thought into Chinaza mind about them asking to wash up after the meal. He also relayed the message that King Runmari would never believe they'd attempt to swim away from him. They hoped the same guard would be the only one joining them. 'But what if he watches our every move?' Chinaza thought. 'I have an idea of how we can distract him,' Oban thought. With that, Chinaza made a request to the guard, who immediately looked over to King Runmari for approval or denial. King Runmari stretched his neck up and over to view the river beside their current camp site. He didn't trust the children but knew that unless they were descendants of fish, they would not be able to cross it. Once again, King Runmari waved and his guard swiftly obeyed.

With Oban's instructions, the three labored over to the water as if too full to move. He advised Chinaza and Badu to appear casual as not to give anything away. Once they were all by the water, Oban asked Chinaza to drop the reeds on the ground so he and Badu could simply pick them up. Further, he told them that even if the guard witnessed this, he would not think anything of it. To Chinaza's delight, when she dropped the twigs, the guard was looking at the sun as it touched the water's edge. Next, Chinaza, at Oban's advice, tripped on purpose over a tree stump. The guard quickly ran to help her up. That was when both Oban and Badu, placed the reeds in their mouths, held their breaths, and went directly into the water. Badu struggled at first. He felt like he wanted to choke, but managed somehow to not make a sound for fear of getting caught.

Now, it was Chinaza's turn. Although she knew what she had to do, she suddenly felt as if she lacked the courage for it. This would be far and away from her comfort. She couldn't believe that Oban had told her that in order to distract the guard, she would have to flirt with him. 'Of all the things to do? Flirt?' she thought, 'With him?' Oban giggled, then placed a thought in her mind, 'You need a way to disappear undetected.' Chinaza grimaced. She would rather him to her to stab the guard instead. Oban giggled again and this time placed another thought, 'No time for that.'

Though, Chinaza hadn't the time to do so, she took a moment to think of any other way to accomplish this feat. Given all she had been through, all she'd seen, she honestly felt like her heart was failing her. It was a devastating feeling. One, she wasn't used to. Then, after contemplating her options, she finally came to the conclusion that Oban was right. She'd seen men do all sorts of foolish things for other girls, women. Truthfully, she just didn't think that any man would act that way for her. She always thought herself too plain to matter. She quickly snuck a peak behind her. To her surprise, both Oban and Badu had already made it into the water. So, with all of her doubts about her womanliness, and realizing that time was running out, she knew she had to go. She had to act quickly less be trapped with this menacing army forever. Then, she reminded herself that after losing her father and brothers, she still managed to save village after village even though that wasn't her original intent. Plus, she did so with the vicious Kenneth army still larking around Degnal Kingdom.

So, with that fresh thought in mind, she collected herself and finally stood firm. She steeled herself, determined to charm the guard, even if it meant playing a part she hated. Suddenly, a surge of energy sparked within her. It was a mixture of fear, anger, defiance, but of all, determination.

CHAPTER 11.

"What this mean, 'This won't end well…'?" Kena asked, quoting the Queen to her mistress once they were completely alone.

Kena made sure of it by checking every corner of the chamber three times each and by standing at the door listening to hear footsteps of anyone who might be eavesdropping on them. Asha hadn't said a word since they left her Queen Mother's presence. She had angrily stomped around the castle, through the corridors into her own chamber like a whirlwind. If she wasn't in such a delicate state, she would have left a slew of broken vases, and dislodged paintings that had been ripped from the walls throughout the palace.

Presently, she was sulking in her cozy chair by the fire; her arms clasped together, her mind raced with thoughts of her grave condition. She hadn't raised her head since they walked in and didn't even acknowledge Kena's existence let alone her query. Discovering that her mistress had not heard her, Kena reached for the tea kettle and gently placed it on the fire. She hoped that with a strong brew, her mistress' tensions would surely ease. Alas, she was so busy with her preparations; she nearly missed Asha's next words; for they were so faint.

"She must be gotten rid of…" Asha finally mouthed, "...That is what that means."

Kena had never heard Asha say a single harsh word against the Queen! It chilled her to her very core. She became so afraid that she ran to the chamber door once more to make doubly sure that the guards hadn't stirred. She feared they might come in at any moment and take them both to the dungeon or worse.

"Maybe we shouldn't speak of such…" Kena said so low that even she could barely hear herself.

"This is serious, Kena…" Asha said through hushed tones and tears, "...my baby's life is at stake!"

Kena knelt at Asha's feet and wept with her. She knew that Asha was under a tremendous strain and honestly wished there was more she could do for her. So, she began rubbing her ankles humming softly a melody that Asha enjoyed, a soothing tribal tune that Asha knew and loved hearing. When she looked up, Asha was smiling warmly at her. Kena felt pride in knowing that she could comfort her so.

"You know exactly what I need, don't you, Kena?"

Asha asked.

Kena merely nodded and continued with the rhythm and the massaging. Asha lay back in her seat and soaked in the soothing treatment. In was indeed most welcome for her and as she quickly discovered it was also good for the baby as well. She could feel the little one moving vigorously as if it were dancing.

"Feel this," Asha said picking up Kena's hand and placing it upon her belly.

"Oh!" Kena giggled, "He's strong."

"He is a mighty warrior…" Asha told her, "...Just like…"

Asha's words trailed off. Suddenly, she felt as if she didn't wish to confide in her only ally, Kena. She pulled away from Kena and eyed her curiously.

"Who have you told, Kena?" Asha barked, "Who? Tell me at once."

Kena leaned back sitting on her hindquarters and wept desperately.

"Mistress…Mistress…Mistress…" she cried, "...I would never, never…"

"Tell me, wench…" Asha demanded, "...You know better than to lie to me!"

Kena bowed her head as low to the ground as she possibly could, "Kill me…" she simply said, "...Kill me, please, if you believe I would ever do such a deceitful thing."

Asha watched Kena wallowing as if in extreme agony for many moments before softening her stance and easing her anger.

"Who then?" Asha asked.

"The Queen Mother has great wisdom," Kena said practically from a prostrate position.

When Asha felt as if Kena had suffered enough, she brought her hand down upon Kena's head gently conveying to her that she could rise again. Kena used the bottom of her dress to wipe away her tears. Her face was red and swollen with welts upon it from the floor.

"Now, now, Kena, you know that you are my most trusted and loyal servant, do you not?" Asha tried to say as convincingly as she could.

"Yes, Mistress Asha," Kena replied.

"Well, now that that is settled…" Asha began, "...I need your assistance."

"Yes, Mistress…" Kena told her, "...Anything."

Kena couldn't wait to be of service to Asha again. She would have done anything for her especially now. She would prove to her that she did not betray her.

"Now, that we have a complete understanding with one another, I have a favor to ask," Asha said.

"Anything, Mistress. Anything…" Kena said, "...You need but ask and I will obey. Anything. Please, Mistress, ask me, your most trusted servant."

"Well, Kena, you do realize that the future King of Degnal's life is at stake?" Asha asked.

"Ask, Mistress…" Kena told her, "...You have but to ask and I will obey."

Asha looked into Kena's willing eyes and knew that she would do anything for her, that she loved her and wanted only for her happiness. Asha knew that about Kena and was grateful to have her.

Asha simply told her, "You must kill the Queen Mother - before the new moon."

CHAPTER 12. In one of the southernmost parts of the Great Lands was a Kingdom called Negi. It was an absolute marvel, one of the most picturesque settlements in the entire world. It had lush green fields, with all manner of tropical trees; including palms, and other exotic varieties. Plus, it held all manner of plant and wild life. The entirety of this land resembled the plushest of gardens. Yet, its uniqueness mainly sprung from the fact that the whole territory sat upon water. It was a beautifully woven cluster of islands within an enormous inlet. Negi's palace, built of red painted stone, was an astonishing grand site at the kingdom's center. Surrounding it were many structures each was brightly adorned in pastel hues. At a distance, this floating metropolis looked like a decorative ring. The palace was its giant ruby setting and the villages around it sparkling like multi-colored diamonds.

Negi Kingdom was not only breathtakingly beautiful; it was also an engineering wonder. It was technologically far and away beyond any other kingdom in the Great Lands, including the likes of Degnal. Inhabitants primarily moved about by way of small vessels maneuvering through a series of narrow but well carved canals.

Connecting these water ways were bridges built out of clay and iron that arched across from island to island. This elaborate system of transport was equipped with aqueducts too for drinking water and even public hot springs and spas. Plus, as stunning as Negi was, it was fortified as well. Enemies of Negi would rather retreat than have to confront its fierce army. They would have already faced a rough, often raging sea before confronting Negi's combat forces.

Ekon, a strappingly handsome, bronze complexioned young man of nineteen winters, was one of Negi's bravest warriors. Since infancy, he was meticulously reared in the hope of becoming one of Negi's favorite sons. His father, the King's goat herder, together with his mother, the chief palace baker, made sure of it. After working to near exhaustion each day, his father would then train Ekon in horse riding, hand-to-hand combat as well as with the sword, and axe. While his mother taught him to read, write, table manners, and social graces. With such attention to Ekon's upbringing, his parents couldn't be prouder of their son. For he was now one of Negi's army highest ranking lieutenants. Ekon had exceeded all expectations of his humble parentage and developed into an exceptional fighter. It was well known that enemies dared to follow a Negian warrior through the sea, but Ekon had become the warrior enemies feared most, the one they'd have to face if they dared. He rose to be known as one of the best at quickly dispatching the likes of any trespasser.

With such an impressive reputation, King Negi took note of Ekon's exceptional prowess and one summer bestowed upon him one of his greatest of honors. Besides gold, silver and land, he gave Ekon his daughter, Mari, to marry. Ekon and his family were overjoyed, and gladly accepted the King's great gifts. Within days, Ekon and Mari were wed. It occurred on a raft that lazily sailed throughout the kingdom in a grand celebration that lasted twenty days and twenty nights.

Ekon was indeed embarking on a bright future. However, there was one small problem. He was not in love with Mari. He had only married her to please his parents; after all they had sacrificed so much for him. He felt indebted to them. Besides, he figured that the marriage wouldn't be completely disagreeable. There were obvious advantages in being the son-in-law to the King; wealth, status, and lifelong comfort. Not to mention, his parents could finally be elevated out of the King's service and into their own deeded property akin to other upper-class citizens.

Another fringe benefit was the fact the Mari was exceptionally beautiful. Also, Ekon truly believed that once his estate was firmly established, he'd be free to do what he loved best, roam throughout the Great Lands as Negi's hero. It never occurred to him that King Negi had other plans in mind for him.

In fact, as soon as the marital festivities were over, King Negi commanded Ekon to immediately cease his exploits. Ekon was completely unaware of King Negi's extreme paranoia and obsession with the Negi lineage. After all, his greatest warrior needed to stay home and produce plenty of descendants for the Negi Kingdom, hadn't he? It didn't matter that none had any chance of ever becoming king. King Negi nonetheless insisted on having a fortified bloodline. He feared that without one the longevity of his Kingdom would be in jeopardy. King Negi believed that a Negi should always sit upon the throne. He was so anxious about the future of his family name, that he maintained a minimum of no less than one-hundred wives at all times, each of child-bearing age. When one of them outlived their usefulness, he'd simply give them the task of nursing his voluminous offspring.

Unfortunately for Ekon, with each full moon, he

grew increasingly weary with the duties of his homebound husbandry. This imposed confinement so saddened him that he eventually began deeply melancholy. The very nature of being tied to the Kingdom in this way was simply unbearable for him. Early into his relationship with Mari, Ekon felt a longing within that could not be denied. He was an adventurer at heart and desired more than anything to be free to explore. He had never been so confined in all his days. He felt as if he'd been imprisoned.

Soon, he began exhausting himself finding ways of leaving Negi Kingdom even if only for very short periods of time. One evening he convinced his mother to sell some of her baked goods to surrounding villages on the mainland. He lied to his wife and said that he didn't really wish to accompany his mother, but that she insisted he be by her side. Alas, Ekon's mother did not enjoy traveling. So, after the initial trip, she decided there wouldn't be another. Ekon was crushed. He was counting on making that excursion a regular one. Regrettably, most of Ekon's schemes met the same fate.

Late one night, after Mari had gone to bed, Ekon overheard several men of Negi's army speaking of a reconnaissance mission. Their King was sending them in search of ore. It was one of many materials that Negi did not produce, but imported. King Negi would have preferred if they could mine their own. So, he sent a small troop out to find uninhabited land that was rich in this precious mineral. Upon hearing of this, Ekon simply saddled his horse and followed these men onto the ship heading for the mainland. He didn't know what he would do once there, but he thought that if he didn't take advantage of this opportunity there might not be another.

Negi's army welcomed him and liked the idea of having the extra help. Once at sea, Ekon felt as if he could breathe again. He hadn't realized how suffocating it was not being unable to roam freely as he had his entire life. So, unlike the Negi army who set up camp and slept until morning, Ekon galloped through the night air taking in as much of the surrounding area as he could. He felt exhilarated, revitalized even. He was at one with all he saw. With the Great Ocean on one side and the mountains on the other, he rode on down to the beach wanting desperately never to look back.

As time passed, he and his horse grew thirsty, so Ekon decided to stop by a stream and replenish. He tied his steed to a tree by the water's edge and they both drank their fill. The cool refreshing drink helped immensely, but having stopped, Ekon realized just how tired he had become. He and his horse needed rest after all. He looked around to make sure there were no wild animals about then took a nap upon tall blades of grass.

Moments later, he was abruptly awakened upon hearing a strange noise in the distance. He immediately jumped to his feet on full alert, preparing for what was coming next. Yet, as he listened more intently, he noted that what he was hearing sounded similar to singing. He thought to himself, 'I must be dreaming.' He hadn't been away from Negi Kingdom in many moons and he recognized that he might simply be going mad. He plopped himself back down on the ground and shook his head in quiet reflection. The irony wasn't lost on him that he had battled fiercely as a warrior only to now be betrayed by his own mind.

The sudden sounds of horse hooves approaching snapped him out of that train of thought. It wasn't his imagination after all; someone was indeed coming in his direction. This time, he stood and began easing over towards his horse. That is where his ax and knife were hidden. He slid both out from their hoisters and waited. To his utter surprise, out from beyond the brush came a strikingly beautiful young woman. She looked as natural as the surrounding, hair flowing down around her shoulders, face illuminated in the moonlight and stars. Ekon couldn't be sure, but she looked otherworldly, yet welcoming and calm.

"Hello," she said, but not to Ekon, instead to his horse.

At that point, Ekon was safely hid behind a tree.

"What are you doing out here alone?" she asked Ekon's horse.

She stroked its nose and the horse neighed. Then she reached within her horse's saddle, pulled out a carrot and fed Ekon's horse.

"There you go," she said, "You must be very hungry out here all by yourself."

The horse happily ate as if enjoying the company and the food.

"I can't ride both of you…" she said to the horse, "…but, I can't leave you here either."

"He's mine," Ekon's said, finally popping out and showing himself in full view.

The woman sharply twisted around to see Ekon holding weapons in both his hands. She was so startled, she fell. Ekon raced over to assist. By the time he reached her, she was upright waving a sword at his head. He stopped in his tracks. Then let out a nervous giggle.

"You should not think me funny," she warned him, "I can and will fight you."

Ekon immediately stopped laughing. He didn't think she was in any way comical. In fact, he believed her to be serious and capable of doing exactly what she said, of that he had no doubt. She held her blade like a seasoned professional. And, with that acknowledgement, Ekon lowered his ax and knife and placed them both on the ground before her.

"I was not making fun of you," Ekon told her, "You look every bit fit for fighting," he smiled.

"It's not just looks," she told him, "I am indeed trained."

"Forgive me for giving you the impression that I mean you any harm," Ekon told her, "I didn't know who was conversing with my horse," he grinned widely, but not wide enough to offend.

The young woman stepped back a pace, and expertly

slipped her sword back in its sheath all the while eyeing Ekon suspiciously.

"You're not from around here, are you?" she asked him smugly.

"Why do you say it that way?" Ekon asked.

"I'm familiar with all the colors the warriors wear…" she began, then hesitated at giving too much away.

"Ah, so you know me to be a warrior?" Ekon smiled.

"Of course, I know," she answered indignantly.

"A clever girl…" Ekon said.

"Girl!" she snapped, "I am not some little girl. If you really knew, you would lower yourself to the ground."

Ekon humbly bowed before her. He would recall this precise moment later as the time he fell in love with her. There was something in her tone that captivated him. He knew he had to get to know everything about her. He already knew that she would someday own his heart.

"My sincerest apologies," he said, "There I go offending you again."

He decided to demonstrate his sincerity further, and dropped down onto one knee. She shrugged as if to say, 'That's better.' He smiled despite himself, quickly covering it up with a cough.

"May I, your humble servant, ask your name?" Ekon asked.

"You may ask and I may refuse to answer," she told him coyly.

Ekon stood up and took a few steps back so that he did not scare her off. He had already decided in his mind that she would be his new reason for desiring to leave Negi Kingdom.

"What is your name?" Ekon asked the woman who he would have loved to make his wife.

She looked at Ekon as if for the first time. There he stood relaxed and disarming awaiting her answer. Dare she say, he seemed somewhat charming to her in that stance. She hadn't noticed before, but he was also exceedingly handsome, skin baked bronze in the sun, slim muscular build, and hair in twists surrounding a chiseled face.

"I am Princess Asha," Asha simply told him.

Little did either of them know, but they would soon become each other's closest allies and so much more.

CHAPTER 13. With their narrow escape still fresh in their minds, Chinaza, Oban and Badu now found themselves floating through a small canal. None of them had any notion where they were. Whilst frightened, and on edge, and although they had to maintain caution, they were exceedingly grateful. In the Great Lands, it wasn't common to flee with one's life from a battalion of bloodthirsty men. These three youths were very fortunate.

In this remote part of the sea, the water was tranquil. So calm and warm, a barrage of tiny fish accompanied them, bumping into their bodies, and tickling the surface of their skin. These creatures were like heavenly guides leading them into a peculiar and welcoming state of peace. All except Badu, of course, who regarded the little beasts as unnerving and disquieting. In fact, Badu found the whole business of being in water altogether troubling. And, it wasn't just because he wasn't allowed to put his head above it, though that was certainly a factor. No, his discomfort stemmed mostly from an acute awareness that earlier that very day, he nearly got them all killed. This occurred during the time Chinaza was formulating their getaway plan.

As soon as Chinaza conveyed the details about how

they should travel under water, Badu could clearly hear his father's voice saying, "You will surely sink to the bottom. You're just too big." Badu had never wanted his father's words to be truer than at that very moment. In fact, he was praying to the gods that they would be. Unfortunately, he realized far too late that his father's words were most assuredly incorrect. Badu was mortified to learn that he could scarcely keep his feet beneath the surface let alone submerging his whole body. To his horror, he could only manage to float on top of the water! And, with that shocking revelation, he panicked, and began splashing about frantically. He was desperately trying to figure out a way to descend. Then, adding to him dismay, his head kept bobbing up no matter how hard he tried to lower it. If it weren't for Chinaza's swift actions of pulling him downward, King Runmari would have immediately discovered their whereabouts. Badu was so ashamed knowing that all would have been lost because of him. He could have sworn he heard his family's laughter ringing in his ears. Now that they were finally safe, he reflected upon his cowardice and felt ashamed and embarrassed.

As the three continued to glide beneath the water, Oban sent Badu a thoughtful message, 'It wasn't your fault.'

Though Badu was relieved to hear him say so, he dared to believe it. In truth, he wouldn't blame either one of them if they never spoke to him ever again. Chinaza looked over and saw Oban giving Badu a reassuring grin. It surprised her that she was somewhat moved by their affection toward one another. Before she knew it, she was smiling as well. She couldn't remember the last time she felt that way - genuinely happy. She reflected on how utterly remarkable it was that they had managed to get away from the clutches of King Runmari. It wasn't at all lost on her that had they remained with him she would have been the solitary female amongst a hoard of beastly, grotesque men. Chinaza wasn't a woman of the world, but she was not naive either. She knew that men had all kinds of appetites, many that only a woman could fulfill. She had no desire to find out what theirs' were, and not just because of their dank breaths and smelly farts. After all, she was raised in a large family of brothers, and though she loved and missed them dearly, she would never miss the enormity of work that accompanied her fairer sex. The feeding, caring for, and household chores sometimes made her regret being born female.

Just then, out of the corner of her eye, Chinaza began

observing the movement of the water. To her delight, she could see that they might actually be approaching land. She could see the depth slowly decreasing, and even saw some vegetation. As she was thinking this, Oban was listening to her thoughts and also began looking around as well, observing the same. They were all thrilled at the prospect of getting out of the water, but also apprehensive about what they might find.

Chinaza poked her head up first. She was the only one amongst them who was an experienced swimmer. She tilted her head slowly sideways, in case hostel forces were about, and then peered forward. She could see what looked like an island straight in front of them only one hundred arms lengths ahead. She briefly dipped her face back under water and nodded to Oban and Badu. Then without hesitation, she tossed her reed aside, kicked her feet and swam in the direction of what she considered pure salvation. It took Oban a mere breath to follow suit. Badu, however, remained submerged, breathing safely through his reed. He'd accomplished more than he thought possible so far. He didn't want to spoil all his effort by now drowning.

Meanwhile, Chinaza, and Oban splashed about and in no time reached the shore. They couldn't believe their good fortune – land at last. Almost immediately they stretched out on the soft, dry sand and allowed their bodies to be gently baked by the sun. Before long, they were both fast asleep. After all that had transpired, they were exhausted. The long journey of running for their lives had finally taken its toll. When Badu finally emerged from the water, he did likewise, collapsing beside them and closing his eyes.

Unfortunately, just as the sun was setting, Oban and Badu were abruptly awakened by Chinaza. She didn't have to give them a reason. For while they peacefully slept, an army of a different sort had now surrounded them. Right there before them, in every direction, were little furry animals. All with their big eyes staring straight at them.

"Ah…," Badu said calmly, "…They're meerkats," he told Chinaza and Oban, "They're harmless."

Chinaza and Oban watched Badu curiously as he quickly leaped up to go over and pet one of them.

"Stop!" Chinaza shouted.

Badu froze in place though he didn't understand why Chinaza was so hesitant around these fuzzy, little creatures.

"I do not believe that they are as harmless as you say, Badu," Oban warned.

Badu giggled at the thought, but when he turned back around to face them, his opinion quickly changed. Every single beast was now displaying all of their ferociously sharp teeth.

"Yikes!" Badu shrieked in horror.

Now, with extreme stealth, Badu slowly began backing away from the animals. As he did so, one of them lurched to bite his yet still extended fingers. He looked around now frightened beyond his wits. He couldn't understand it. He had these same animals in his village where they were kept as pets. He had never seen them look so ferocious. Then, like a trained army, the meerkats started marching closer and closer to all three of them.

"Do something!" Badu shouted to Chinaza and Oban.

"What?" Chinaza asked, "We haven't a weapon!"

The animals were slobbering spit as if they were ravenously hungry for flesh.

"Do something! Quick!" Badu exclaimed again.

He was the closest to the horrible critters and feared that his sheer girth was making their mouths water. He cursed every meal he'd ever eaten. He'd made it this far, through the ocean no less, only to be devoured by, what he considered for years, his four-legged friends.

"Do something, now!" he pleaded, "We're about to be…Oh, no…no….!"

One of the animals nearest to him lunged and knocked him down to the ground. Badu managed by a hair to block its protruding fangs just as they were about to clamp down on his neck. He quickly managed to roll in the sand from one side to the other trying desperately to protect himself. Meanwhile, the other animals raced around towards Chinaza and Oban. Chinaza and Oban did all they could to prepare themselves for the attack but the only thing they could do was tuck their heads beneath their arms. Unfortunately, the meerkats rushed over and mauled them as well. There were just too many of them. Soon, all that could be seen was a giant ball of dirt and dust. The three fought valiantly, but the animals were so fierce that they managed to bite and scratch them anyway.

Oban's spirits sank so much that his thoughts began to drift as his flesh was being gnawed on by the meerkats. Once more, he longed to see his home, beautiful Degnal Kingdom with its majestic mountains, and picturesque gardens. He feared that with all he'd been through, he might never see it again. Sadness crept up inside his inner most being and began to consume him. Ironically, this ache inside shielded him against the pain he was enduring. He was being swallowed alive. His suffering was so acute that eventually he cried out because of it. Yet no sound came from his lips. It was a hollow, burning sensation in the pit of his stomach. That intense grief quickly shifted to outright rage. He couldn't believe that his father, the King, had not come to rescue him in all these long terrible days. 'Why do I even want to go home?' he wondered.

"For what?" he yelled, but this time it out came in a roar as loud as a lion.

At once, a pack of wild carnivorous wolves began to swarm the beach. It appeared as if they came out of nowhere. Then the wolves slowly surrounded the meerkats. The meerkats immediately stopped attacking the three friends and instead froze in place. Oban, Chinaza, and Badu could barely move for the pain, and now panic, but mostly for the sheer wonder of what was happening. As they looked out as far as their eyes could see, they now saw wolves charging towards them. Some came from the trees, some from behind boulders, and some looked as if they came out the Great Ocean. Oban placed a thought into Chinaza and Badu's minds, to back away from the meerkats

- slowly, he warned them, very slowly. The three slid as carefully as possible from under and around their attackers, and steadied themselves for what was coming next. Alas, there wasn't really anywhere else for them to go. They found themselves quite literally in the middle of two sets of menacing animals. With no time or place to flee, the three huddled together in a tight ball and shut their eyes. Unfortunately, Oban could clearly hear what Chinaza and Badu were thinking, 'We're going to die! We're going to die! WE'RE GOING TO DIE!'

Oban, though weary, wasn't thinking about death at all. In fact, that was the furthest thing from his mind. He was still fuming over the fact that he had been stolen away in the middle of the night in the first place, from an armed fortress, to boot. Everything he was going through was due to that single event, including his current circumstance. He still couldn't understand how someone managed to whisk him out of his chamber without him even sensing their presence. Normally, he could have been awakened by hearing other people's dreams! Then there was the issue of where he was taken to, he thought, 'To the worst place on earth!'

Oban couldn't contain his rising temper any longer.

He stood up and began screaming at the top of his lungs. This time, a loud guttural sound came from his mouth. Yet, it seemed to emanate from his entire body. And, the more Oban yowled; more and more wolves descended upon the beach.

Chinaza and Badu paid little attention to Oban, as they were too frightened to lift their heads. But, eventually Chinaza peaked to see what was going on around her. When she did, she couldn't believe what she saw. She blinked several times over and over again. It was so peculiar and unreal. She couldn't be sure if she were even awake. It all seemed to be happening as if in a dream. She looked out once more, but this time forced Badu to do the same. They were both in shock.

There right along the shore was Oban marching in front of an enormous pack of wolves. Astonishingly, he looked as if he were leading them away from Chinaza and Badu without making a single sound. There, in the wolves' mouths were the meerkats' broken bodies. Not a single one was left in the sand.

"Their dinner," Chinaza whispered.

Badu nodded in agreement, suddenly realizing that they hadn't eaten in all this time. At that, Oban turned and faced one of the wolves. The wolves immediately stopped walking, dropped his meerkat and dove headfirst into the ocean. Moments later he arose carrying a very large fresh salmon in his teeth. The wolf then proceeded to carry the fish over to the ever increasingly stunned Chinaza and Badu. The wolf plopped his haul at their feet, then about faced, retrieved his meal and continued along with his kind. Chinaza and Badu stood frozen in place. They didn't make a move, not even when Oban finally made his way back over to them. In truth, they both were trying to determine who they were more frightened of; the meerkats, the wolves or their dear friend, Oban.

CHAPTER 14. Unbeknownst to Chinaza, Badu, or Oban, someone had been watching their every move that day out there on that seemingly deserted beach. The moment the wolves departed, she revealed herself before them by springing forth so quickly towards them that it appeared as if by magic. The now startled and shaken three huddled together in fright.

"So, what do we have here?" she smirked condescendingly, staring rather intently at Oban specifically.

Oban immediately backed away from her all the while feeling concerned for, he hadn't sensed her at all before she sprung as if out of nowhere. Also, her mere presence before him, made his head hurt.

"No need to do that, child..." the woman grinned, "...You will not be able to take my thoughts out of my head like you so easily do theirs," she spat contemptuously in the direction of Chinaza and Badu.

Oban eyed her cautiously, thinking all the while, 'What is she hiding?'

"Yes, I know who you are," the woman sneered at Oban.

"You know my father?" Oban asked.

"What does your father have to do with it?" the woman disrespectfully barked.

Oban now looked at her curiously, thinking, 'What could she possibly mean by that?'

"You're not very smart, are you?" she shirked.

Oban loathed being grilled like this. He knew he was at a disadvantage; he just didn't know why.

"Do you two intend to eat that fish, or what?" she asked Chinaza and Badu's stricken faces.

Neither Chinaza nor Badu desired to speak with the strange woman - and, not just because of the enormous, knotted, matted, unruly mane atop her head. She would be categorized as a woman from the bushes, surviving in the wild just like the creatures they had just encountered. Evidence of their assessment of her was her small frame covered with at least four layers of clothing, some animal skins and something that could quite possibly have been tree bark. As they were summing up her attributes, she sharply turned and faced them both, staring as if she might strike them at any given moment. Chinaza and Badu felt as if they were being picked apart far worse than the meerkats. Then, as their fear swelled, the odd woman suddenly burst into raucous laughter, while glaring at Oban, "Why are you with these little pests?"

"Do not speak rudely of my friends," Oban demanded half-heartedly trying desperately to summon his rightful authority as the son of a king.

"Or what?" she grinned, "Friends? More like dust under my feet."

Chinaza stepped towards her, but Oban placed a thought in her mind, not to do so.

"I see you have them well trained," the woman smiled.

Then the woman pointedly backed away from the three giving them space. All at once, her countenance was dramatically changed. She went from being the menacing foreigner to 'of all the strange things,' the gracious host.

"Well, you three must be hungry, yes?" she welcomed them.

Without awaiting an answer, she started walking inland, and then without turning back them, "You coming?" she asked over her shoulder.

"We can fend for ourselves," Chinaza said boldly picking up the salmon.

"If you'd like to see what animals roam at night, be my guests," the woman said still strolling away from them.

Moments later, she glanced behind her and found the three friends following her. Neither Chinaza, Oban, nor Badu trusted her, but they knew she was right. It wasn't safe for them to be out in the open by the shore. They had already discovered that nuance firsthand. They realized that they didn't have much of a choice. Having no idea where they were, they figured that some help was far better than none at all. So, they trailed behind the peculiar woman and hoped she'd lead them towards Degnal and away from danger.

As they climbed up a large sand bank and all they saw were fields of tall grass and not much else. Chinaza, Badu and Oban stood, mouths agape wondering just where they were. Their hearts sank. It seemed apparent that civilization was a long way off.

"Quickly now," the woman said, "You have to follow closely in these parts. We don't want to wake up the snakes."

"Snakes?" Badu yelped.

"Are you hard of hearing?" she snapped, "Yes, snakes!"

Then the woman took off running through the blades of grass in a dizzying zigzag pattern. Surprisingly, Badu managed to keep up with her best. In fact, he was nearly on her heels. Of a great many fears he possessed, the slivering kind was at the top of his long list. Chinaza and Oban nearly laughed out loud when he whizzed past them. Badu was going to make sure he didn't lose their eccentric woman of that, he was sure. He knew that he couldn't afford to get lost.

After a lengthy run, they were all out of breath by the time their guide stopped. And, directly ahead of them stood a large cabin of sorts.

"Home," the woman said.

Chinaza, Oban and Badu looked in the direction of her "home" and couldn't figure why she would describe it as such. There didn't seem to be anything that suggested the familiar. Best they could determine, it was a rundown shack and that was when the sunlight hit it. The structure hadn't any recognizable shape at all. The top was a combined patchwork of various types of giant leaves seemingly adhered with some type of slimy goo. There wasn't a doorway in sight. The three friends thought hard about how she got in and out of the thing. A stack of fallen trees were on one side and the remaining walls, if one could refer to them as such, consisted of either rocks and/or droopy mud.

Twigs poked out in every direction, clearly meant to be perches for birds. The place was surrounded by all types of flying creatures.

Then the strange woman walked into her equally strange house and bade the three friends follow. They hesitantly obeyed because they hadn't the strength to turn around and face neither the snakes nor the tall grass again. Besides, they were hungry and exhausted from all that had befallen them. So, very carefully, they stepped where she trod over dried leaves, marsh, branches and the like. Then, without much confidence, they entered the domicile. Nothing could have prepared them for what they saw inside.

Chinaza, Oban and Badu stood frozen at the entrance, completely shocked by what they saw.

"It's…," Chinaza began.

"It's…," Oban tried.

"It's...lovely," Badu blurted out while cheerfully scanning every inch of the house.

"What did you expect?" asked the woman defensively, as she walked over to a brick fire pit that already had wood burning in it.

To the three friends' astonishment, the place was toasty warm and welcoming, and unlike anything they'd ever seen. It was quite a striking surprise from what they imagined it would be from the likes of outside. Instead of a rundown hut, it was by all accounts, a mansion. The rough exterior kept well hid the grand marble columns posted within, supporting a ceiling that replicated the night sky. It actually sparkled like stars. There was a large woven fabric decorating the walls in vibrant colors matching a cluster of sofas partitioned off in a seating area.

"Sit!" the woman barked, then, "Please."

The three immediately obeyed. And, as they sat, the animal skin chairs seemed to swaddle their bodies in comfort. The woman walked over to Chinaza.

"Chinaza, would you like me to cook the fish for you?" the woman asked her.

"Yes, plea…." Chinaza replied, and then her eyes widened, "How did you know my name?"

She smiled gently and took the salmon out of Chinaza's hands.

"I know all of your names," the woman informed them.

Abruptly, all three stood up and readied themselves to run out of the woman's house.

"Sit," the woman said placing the fish in a pan and

then onto the fire, “You already know of one who can do as I do.”

The three friends begrudgingly sat back down.

“What do you mean?” Badu reluctantly asked.

“You really are not very bright, are you?” the woman asked Badu.

She then placed a thought into Oban’s mind, ‘Tell them, Oban. Tell them what I can do.’ At that, Oban stiffened in his seat.

“But…but…but…” Oban stuttered.

“But you cannot hear my thoughts. Can you?” the woman asked.

“No, no,” Oban said, “I cannot,” he admitted.

“You have not been taught well at all,” the woman told him disapprovingly.

“I hadn’t anyone to teach me anything about this. I was told to keep it secret,” Oban explained defensively.

“I see,” the woman said, “So, you don’t even know what you are, do you?”

“I do not,” Oban confessed.

The woman shrugged her shoulders, continued cooking and looked far off lost in thought.

“So, what am I?” Oban hesitantly asked.

The woman turned her gaze to meet Oban's wide-eyed stare.

"You are a thought thief, of course," the woman simply told him.

Oban lowered his head and contemplated her words, 'thought thief.' He had never stolen a thing in his life and didn't like the idea of being someone who's very nature did such things.

"And, that makes you…?" Oban asked.

"Oh, I am one as well," the woman said proudly, "It's a gift."

"A gift?" Oban asked curiously.

That would not be the way he'd describe it.

"Then how would you describe it?" the woman asked upon hearing his thoughts.

"I don't know…" Oban began, "...The idea of taking anything from anyone is…"

"...Is who we are…" the woman told him, "Get used to it because that is exactly who we are."

Oban felt forlorn at the prospect. Before the woman spoke the words, 'thought thief' he realized that all this time, he was sincerely trying to be like everyone else. If he, had it his way, he'd stop the thoughts from flying into his head altogether.

"Bite your tongue!" the woman exclaimed.

Meanwhile, Chinaza and Badu merely looked on at the woman and especially at Oban. They knew full well their disadvantage in this conversation. They could only determine that most of what was being said was with thoughts.

"You really do not know anything, do you?" the woman asked Oban.

"How could I?" Oban replied, "There wasn't anyone like me around to tell me."

"Yes…yes," the woman agreed, "I thought I was the last one."

"I don't even know who you are. You already know our names. What is yours'?" Oban asked her, "If you don't mind telling us."

"I'm Enithan," she answered.

Both Chinaza and Badu nodded a greeting. Oban gave her a tight-lipped grin. He felt very unsettled about being something other than just a normal boy. Plus, he didn't like the idea of having any similarities to this woman.

"You may not want anything to do with me, but I can teach you a few things…if you like…" Enithan told

Oban, "...much more than just ordering those wolves to protect you."

"He did that?" Badu asked.

"Of course, he did! He's like me," Enithan said, "We can do much more than that too."

"Wow!" Badu exclaimed.

"You saved us again," Chinaza said partially smiling at Oban.

Oban looked blanched. He didn't know quite how to feel about being akin to the strange woman before him. He didn't want his friends to think him any odder than they already did.

"Did I?" Oban asked mostly to himself.

"When you're ready, you can command armies," Enithan said quietly.

CHAPTER 15. A meager handful of Kenneth's soldiers had just returned from Degnal. Before consorting with anyone in the villages, they went directly to the Council of Elders, who were gathered at Elder Isoba's home. With heavy hearts and humbled spirits, they delivered the bad news. Before long, it dawned on the Council that standing before them might be all that was left of their entire army. Thankfully, this few managed to escape with their lives from what they had been told was an utterly brutal battle that had taken place at Degnal Castle.

"We were caught unawares!" one shrieked painfully.

"It was like they knew all about the spell," another told them.

"We were surrounded. They were even more powerful than any of the stories about them had been told to us," the third one lamented.

The Kenneth Elders were greatly grieved by the soldiers' words. They couldn't help but feel utterly defeated. Not only was the elixir worthless, but one of them would have to give their life for it, but now they'd lost presumably all the men of Kenneth in one deadly campaign.

Plus, on top of everything, they hadn't the satisfaction of avenging their maimed brethren, the main purpose. Nothing they wished to accomplish had been done. Even so, Priest Godlumthakathi was coming to collect his harsh payment - one of their heads.

Suddenly, there was a pounding on the door so weighty that the walls actually shook. Next followed a great roar outside. Given the information the Elders just heard, they couldn't imagine who it could be. For Priest Godlumthakathi hadn't any need to break the door down in order to get to one of them. His magic was otherworldly and completely capable of moving freely about through mortar, brick and clay. Besides, he didn't seem to be in any rush.

"Who could that be?" Elder Duna asked his comrades.

None wished to respond, especially when it came to answering the door. They were in various stages of panic. Elders Nafari and Sam anxiously remained seated. Their minds raced and their hearts steadily thumped over what they had just heard from the soldiers. They were the two who were the most apprehensive at the very beginning when war with Degnal was even suggested. Each kept muttering to themselves words like, "All is lost," "We are doomed," "What is to become of us?" Finally Elder Isoba rose, took a deep breath and bravely walked to the front door. Once there, he contemplated his fate, then wiped sweat from his brow with his sleeve and unlatched the closer. He hadn't a clue of what or who was about to greet him. He thought, 'Is it too much to ask that it be the rest of the army?'

"Hello," he said pulling the door open and sighing sadly at what he saw.

There before him stood an enormous throng of women. He couldn't be sure, but it looked as though the entire Kenneth female population was standing there staring at him. Unfortunately, he knew all too well why they were there. It was customary in Kenneth for messengers to return and report on the battles, exploits, and travels, and the like, whenever one of their kin left the territory. What was not custom was for the messenger to be detained so long with the Council of Elders. From this, the Kenneth women knew that there had to be something that had gone horribly wrong. By this time in the morning, they would have already heard all about the happenings. So, there they all were, gathered before Elder Isoba's home, demanding answers.

"Where is my husband, Elder Isoba? You told us all that this was a sure victory?" one wife asked.

She had four little children surrounding her, pulling at the hem of her dress.

"Yes, and mine too? Why are they not back yet?" another shouted.

The rest of the Elders came to the entrance and were now facing a mob of tired, disgruntled Kenneth women.

"We are just now getting the information you seek…" Elder Dana interjected.

His lie immediately received a slew of perturbed raised eyebrows from his fellow Elders. They never, ever resorted to lying. That just wasn't their way. However, given their current circumstance, none felt inclined to correct Elder Dana. He gave each one of them a glance before continuing to speak to the Kenneth women. If any of his brothers were to correct him, he would have stepped aside. None did, so he continued.

"...It's a bit more complicated than we expected and…and…and we're going to need more time…" he said.

"More time?" a woman yelled, "Why is that? When are they coming home? That is all we want to know!"

The surprised look of concern on all the Elders'

faces nearly gave away their delay tactic. All the Elders shot a look at Elder Isoba, who immediately felt pressured to come up with a better scenario that would satiate their Kenneth women. He was, after all, the Elder that they all looked up to the most in times of trouble. Being the eldest of the Elders, he knew he had to say something, but he was the worst liar of the bunch. He really and truly didn't know what he could possibly do to remedy this situation.

"Well…well…well…" he stammered, "...The Degnal army is no match for us, of course..." he tried miserably, "...So, our men are overwhelmed…I mean to say…"

"Burdened…" Elder Dana jumped in, "...burdened…with the gathering up of such a great deal of spoils!"

The word 'spoils' came out of Elder Dana's mouth like a war cry. It was the only thing he could think of at the time. He regretted it right away because it was absolutely the wrong thing to say. Immediately, the crowd erupted with cheers. They were so loud and ruckus, the Elders took a few steps back from the sheer force of the shouts. Then the women hugged one another expressing tears of joy, patting each other on the back and giggling in celebration.

"Go home, Kenneth women, and await word from us by…by morning," Elder Isoba managed to say over the din of excitement.

Eventually, the Kenneth women cheered once more than happily dispersed to their several homes. As soon as they had all vanished and the coast was clear, the Elders filed back into Elder Isoba's domicile. It was still early morning, yet they each looked long - faced and exhausted. None spoke a word for a goodly length of time.

Finally, when they looked up, they remembered that the army messengers were still there. The young men were staring at each one of them. They knew that their trusted Elders had just lied through their teeth to their people. The Elders watched them carefully as they stood at attention, gently resting their hands on their weapons. They were soldiers who knew that if a man could blatantly lie, he could also kill to save his own neck just as easily. They knew the truth and could therefore be considered liabilities. The soldiers began slowly walking backward towards the door. They had the advantage both in age and in sheer fighting knowledge, but weren't taking any chances nonetheless.

The Elders didn't protest. They showed more of their cowardice by remaining silent and simply parting a way for them as they exited.

"We see you need time to concoct a better story," one soldier said under his breath, "We'll leave you to it then."

Elder Isoba nodded in agreement for he felt that he hadn't any other choice.

CHAPTER 16. Asha was fuming on account of her father's, King Degnal's, recent proclamation.

"He has the nerve… I cannot believe that he could… What on earth is going on?" Asha ranted.

"Princess Asha, what has happened that has upset you so?" Kena asked a very troubled Asha.

"I'll tell you, Kena, what I'm so angry about," Asha responded without answering the question.

Instead, she sat in her comfortable chair and seethed. Kena didn't know quite what to do to sooth her mistress. She quickly gathered that her presence might not be necessary. Asha was looking down and seemed to be in another world. With nowhere else to go, Kena stood awkwardly. Then she paced the chamber looking for items that might comfort Asha. Having found nothing, she determined that maybe Asha just needed to rest a while. So, she stood very still and simply waited for Asha's breathing to become steadier. Kena knew that when Asha was ready, she'd tell her exactly what took place at the private meeting she just had with her father.

At sunrise, that very morning, Asha was summoned

by the King to get dressed immediately and join him in his chamber. This was not a normal occurrence. The entire occurrence took Asha completely by surprise, especially when she arrived at his door. She was greeted so unceremoniously not only her father, but also by her mother, the Queen. Asha felt blindsided by her presence, so soon after their latest talk. She regretted that she hadn't enacted her scheme to do away with her mother that very day. Now, she realized too late that she had undoubtedly missed her only opportunity.

She could tell right away that her mother had probably already told her father about her condition and that she would have to suffer whatever consequence was about to befall her. What other choice did she have? Little did Kena know, Asha was about to divulge the nature of that conversation, changing both their futures forever.

"Kena, I'm afraid that my offspring will not rule over Degnal in the way I had envisioned after all," Asha began in a barely audible whisper.

"But he will rule nonetheless, right?" Kena asked happily now that Asha was finally calm enough to speak.

"Aye, he will…but…" Asha said mournfully.

The pause was so thick Kena could hardly breathe

because of it. Her heart began to ache for the sorrow she saw in Asha's face. Asha looked white as a ghost. Her bronze glow had turned pale and gray and she appeared frozen like a statue.

"What, Mistress? What?" Kena asked, desperate now for both of them to be taken out of their misery.

"That woman, my beloved mother, has informed the King that I am with child…" Asha said spitting the words bitterly, "...And, that he, my father, the King, apparently needs to do something about it."

"Oh…," Kena said with her heart sinking and her knees buckling beneath her.

As Kena sank to the floor, Asha continued.

"Seems my father, the King of Degnal…" Asha said humorously, "...has devised a plan alright…and it includes you, my dear friend and companion."

"Me?" Kena asked tearfully.

"Yes, you," Asha answered.

If Kena could have melted into the marble tiles she would have done so, but she was already sufficiently dismayed. Their plan of offering up Asha's son as a suitable replacement to her long-lost brother, Oban, was quickly becoming a distance dream.

"My father has decided that he has no other choice but to marry me off, he said," Asha conveyed to Kena matter-of-factly.

"Marry? But to whom?" Kena asked.

"Seems that part was of no real concern to him…" Asha answered, "...It will be someone, he says, suitable to this 'unfortunate predicament' I've placed the 'Kingdom' in, he said. 'Unfortunate predicament?' I was abducted, remember? This is not my fault! With all the military might of his Kingdom, he did not protect me like he said he always would!" she shouted.

"Oh," Kena mouthed in contemplation.

Once again, Asha was angry and unsettled. Kena could do nothing but weep.

"You know what this means, don't you, Kena?" Asha asked mysteriously.

Kena had no idea and truly didn't wish to hear the telling of her fate now that the news of Asha's secret had been revealed.

"Well, I'll tell you…" Asha began, "...It means that both you and I will be carted away from our home to some strange part of the Great Lands, that's what this means," Asha cried.

"Oh!" Kena wailed.

"Oh!" Asha wailed right along beside her.

They were both in agony over the idea of having to leave Degnal Kingdom, the only home either of them had ever known. It was more than they could bear. All they could do was sob at the thought of it.

Yet, in the midst of their sorrow, Asha suddenly lifted her head and, of all things, she managed to smile. Kena looked over at her and didn't know quite what to make of the grin upon her face.

"Have you come up with a plan, Mistress?" Kena asked hopefully.

"Kena, I always have a plan," Asha smirked.

Kena wiped her eyes and tried to muster a smile as well. She failed at it miserably.

"What is it?" she inquired.

"I have one more surprise for my father, the King and his lady, my mother, the Queen…," Asha said cryptically, "...They will not see this one coming. Bring me my riding clothes."

"Yes, Mistress," Kena obeyed, "A ride will do you good."

"We ride together today, Kena. You're coming with

me," Asha told her.

CHAPTER 17. King Runmari rode his horse hard that morning in the direction of Degnal Kingdom. 'Finally,' he thought, 'I am going to have my prized property at last.' He couldn't believe his good fortune yet again. He had had it in his grasp many times and due to unforeseen circumstances, allowed it to slip away. This time it was beyond perfection, and he didn't have to lift a finger in any way to earn it. In fact, it would be handed to him on a silver platter by none other than its King. Oh, King Runmari was all smiles now. Naturally, he did not let his good humor show to his men. To them, he conveyed complete indifference. He believed them incapable of understanding the royal intricacies between kings anyway. In his mind, it was far and away too advanced for their feeble minds.

The circumstances surrounding his contentment had to do with a recent unexpected guest from Degnal Kingdom. As luck would have it, mere days after Oban and his friends fled from his camp, a Degnal messenger came to call upon him. It took a great deal of restraint on the part of King Runmari not to unleash his frustration over Oban's escape on the lowly servant come to call. Luckily for the messenger, certain realities had begun to dawn on King

Runmari of late. For example, he noticed that he needn't lose his temper as often as he had in the past. He discerned that when he did not, he still managed to get what he wanted anyway and without much of a fuss. The current state of affairs more than proved this theory.

"I have a message from the great King Degnal," the messenger pronounced.

King Runmari lowered his raised arm. He had it in the air and was about to strike the man across his face, and then quickly thought better of it. After all, he thought, 'This man did not let Oban get away, but one of my men had.' He would deal with that betrayer soon enough. And, then, out of sheer curiosity, he allowed the man to speak even though he disrespectfully used the word 'great' to describe another king.

"Speak," he hissed at him.

"I have news from King Degnal…" the messenger repeated, "...for King Runmari."

"Well, I am he. Speak!" King Runmari shouted, annoyed of having to repeat himself.

The messenger stepped gingerly forward, eager to tell the message.

"It is for your ears only," the messenger conveyed.

King Runmari removed the blade he was carrying from its sheath in full sight of the messenger. He doubted that King Degnal would send such a small, frail man to do him in, but if that was his purpose, he would be ready. Then he sent his men out of his tent.

"Speak," King Runmari bade in what would be the last time he'd say anything to this servant.

"The great King Degnal wishes an audience with you, King Runmari," the messenger said with a flourish.

King Runmari didn't know what to think about this news. As far as he was concerned, no king ordered him around.

"Why?" King Runmari asked in a perfunctory way.

"The great King Degnal would like to discuss matters of his daughter with you, King Runmari," the messenger continued.

"Matters of his daughter?" King Runmari asked nearly with a chuckle.

The messenger appeared to be finished with the message leaving King Runmari to ponder how on earth he could possibly be of assistance in a conversation with King Degnal about his daughter.

"No, thank you," King Runmari told him flatly and

waved for him to leave.

The Degnal messenger seemed positively confused. Of all the answers, he never considered 'no' to be among them.

"But you don't understand…King Degnal insists that you…" the messenger tried.

"Oh, he insists, does he?" King Runmari grinned.

Fortunately, the messenger immediately realized his mistake. King Runmari stood up and faced the now shaken man. King Runmari towered over him purposely lingering so the man could feel the full weight of his error. The messenger had to raise his head to see King Runmari's dark face. This was not a safe stance to take with the king, but the messenger now felt desperate. He had to get King Runmari to accompany him back to Degnal. If he even appeared to be disobedient to his king, his life would be at stake.

"I believe…" the messenger began.

King Runmari picked up a small paring knife from the table and glared at the messenger. It was so tiny in his large hand that all the messenger saw were his ashy knuckles with a sharp object poking out from underneath.

"...I believe…" the messenger said grabbing at his neck as if to protect it, "...I believe…it may have something to do with a union," the messenger reluctantly blurted.

King Runmari paused momentarily and allowed the messengers words to sink in. 'Union?' he thought. That one word left him utterly stunned. For, that word could mean any number of things, but the essence that stood out for King Runmari was a possible alliance. If, he wanted a marriage, King Runmari had plenty of sons for which King Degnal could choose. On the other hand, he had captured many acres of land in the Great Lands. Perhaps King Degnal was looking to expand his territory. As for silver and gold, neither had need for them, but both owned scores of those niceties as well. In his mind, he realized that far and away, his lot actually rivaled that of King Degnal's. This could be a very advantageous turn of events for King Runmari; an opportunity such as this seldom, nah NEVER came his way. He would be a fool not to at least hear what 'great' King Degnal had to say.

So, that damp morning, King Runmari entered the main gate of Degnal castle for his meeting with King Degnal promptly. Upon arriving, he was greeted by two of the King's trusted Advisors. King Runmari thought of Advisor Burton for a moment. He knew exactly what became of him from an account given by one of his spies. They couldn't say for certain who actually killed Advisor Burton, but they knew that he entered the castle upright and came out of the castle prostrate with a death shroud covering his body.

King Runmari was escorted to the Winter Chamber. It was in a part of the castle for which King Runmari was unfamiliar. The name evoked cold weather and desolation. As he approached the door that was exactly the impression it gave him. The hallway leading to the room had white branches lining the walls, and painted acorns strewn upon the amber colored stone floor. With the symbolism for which Degnal was well known, King Runmari wondered why this particular meeting place was chosen.

The doors of the chamber opened as if by themselves. King Runmari smiled. He did appreciate the Degnal servants and their attention to every detail. Even when King Runmari crossed the threshold into the room, he still did not see anyone at the entrance. He thought that he could get used to that particular trick. The Advisors escorted him down to a long table. There sat King Degnal looking as gray as the sparsely furnished room.

"Welcome, King Runmari," King Degnal said, rising only slightly and extending his hand to an empty chair.

"Thank you," King Runmari said, sitting down.

King Runmari's curiosity was piqued when he saw the Advisors sit as well. He thought the meeting would be solely between Kings. It troubled him somewhat that he was mistaken. As he was mulling that over, the doors of the chamber opened and there upon entered Queen Degnal accompanied by twelve servants following. King Runmari stood despite himself. He wouldn't ordinarily rise for any woman, but there was something about Queen Degnal that seemed to demand such respect.

Queen Degnal floated across the floor, head high, flanked on every side by her entourage who looked a tad tougher than the guards surrounding the King. Once she was seated upon her throne, she gave the smallest of nods to her husband, King Degnal. The gesture was so slight that had King Runmari not been staring directly at her, he would have missed it. He realized that her son, Oban, had inherited his good looks and poise from her alone. She was, in one word, exquisite. Her flawless skin actually glistened. King Runmari looked towards the windows and didn't see any light shining into the dreary room whatsoever. He tried and couldn't discover where her constant radiance was emanating from. Her beautiful, womanly shape could not be denied either even beneath the copious mounds of spun fabric doing its best to cover her up. She was delicate and fierce, timid and forceful, demure and wild like a beast. King Runmari didn't know what to make of her, but he immediately knew a very peculiar notion, he desired her.

"My wife, Queen Degnal," King Degnal said to King Runmari in introduction.

King Runmari had not taken his eyes off of her, and now worried that his intense gawking seemed obvious, and awkward.

"Isn't she the most beautiful of queens?" King Degnal asked with a grin.

'Alas, it does seem obvious,' King Runmari thought, and then said, "Yes. Yes, she is," he managed as nonchalantly as he could muster. All the while wanting desperately to be alone with her. It only took a second, but he was completely smitten and now couldn't stop himself from thinking of no one but her. Ordinarily, any woman would not be a problem for him to take as his wife - ordinarily, but these were not ordinary times. He was a guest in King Degnal's home, his grand castle, his kingdom, surrounded by his grand army. An army, he was just told, destroyed an entire kingdom without losing even one of their own soldiers.

King Runmari thought about that situation, 'I will take Kenneth next. Now, that they are so vulnerable.' Though he hadn't any desire of living there at all in its frigid temperatures, he could offer them protection in exchange for resources. Fortunately for him, they were easy pickings now that there wasn't a single man left standing thanks to King Degnal.

"King Degnal, you've been very busy, I hear," King Runmari probed in hopes of hearing more about Kenneth.

"No doubt you've heard that we were attacked," King Degnal responded without giving any details.

"You make it seem as if you didn't know they were coming?" King Runmari inquired coyly.

Each King was well aware of every minute detail of the assault on Degnal Kingdom as they were both given moment-by-moment reports. Their conversation was merely to keep up appearances. Meanwhile, each knew that each was wary of the other. King Degnal shot King Runmari a look. He had no intension of revealing any of his secrets and therefore, quickly changed the subject.

"So…" King Degnal began, "I requested your presence here and in the sight of my lovely wife and trusted

Advisors to ask you a favor."

"Favor?" King Runmari asked, "How can I possibly be of service to you?"

King Degnal gave a very long look to his wife, Queen Degnal before continuing. She didn't move. King Runmari observed this exchange and wondered why such a dramatic pause. King Degnal finally turned and faced King Runmari. Then with a clenched jaw he spoke.

"It has come to my attention, while my daughter, Asha, was out of my care…" King Degnal paused.

'Out of your care,' King Runmari mused. He nearly rolled his eyes in derision at the King Degnal's minimalistic description of that event. All the Great Land's knew that it was King Degnal's incompetence that allowed his one and only daughter to be taken from his so-called fortified castle. And, of all the humiliation, now his son, Oban, suffered the same fate. King Runmari tried not to let it show but he was thinking of King Degnal as pathetic and careless. He knew that whatever this 'favor' was that he was going to use King Degnal's weakness against him in fulfilling it. Of that, he was sure.

"...she became in a family way…" King Degnal went on.

'Family way?' King Runmari contemplated this for a moment. That scenario hadn't occurred to him. 'So, his daughter was impregnated by her abductors,' King Runmari thought, 'How wonderful.' The great King Degnal was in a vulnerable state. Now, there was concrete evidence of King Degnal's lacking. The Great Land's would know that not only did he let his daughter out of his sight, but he allowed her to be ruined in the process. 'What descent royal family would want the spoiled and soiled brat now?' King Runmari mused.

"...As you can see, I'm in no position to offer her in marriage and, therefore, must employ different tactics for such a delicate situation," King Degnal said.

"Tactics?" King Runmari asked inquisitively.

"Well, yes," King Degnal answered, then paused and concluded with, "...I understand that you have a great many sons?"

King Runmari grinned, thinking, 'Of course, that is why I was summoned.'

"Yes, yes, I do..." King Runmari replied, "...a great many. All strong, virile warriors, trained in combat by my trusted mighty heroes," King Runmari said proudly.

"Yes, well...yes," King Degnal said and paused,

then stopped.

King Runmari waited patiently for King Degnal to ask him out right for this particular courtesy, but quickly noticed that a formal request might never come. In fact, King Degnal lowered his head in shame instead. Still, King Runmari longed to hear King Degnal ask for his help. He would have loved to hear begging from his lips, together with a great many 'thank yous.' Unfortunately, no other words came from the King. Suddenly, the doors of the winter room opened and in walked Asha, the King's daughter. Asha was followed by Kena.

King Runmari was still staring at King Degnal and hadn't yet seen Asha until she approached the throng. When he first gazed upon her, he noted her extremely delicate features. Even more so than Queen Degnal, Asha glided across the floor as if floating too. She was an absolute vision. King Runmari was completely awestruck by her beauty as well. She reminded him of a black swan, regal and poised, rare and exotic. He stood and remained standing as she made her way around to her mother, the Queen. Thankfully, only moments later, he realized that he was the only male still standing while everyone else had already been seated. He closed his mouth, which had been agape the whole time, and tried not to now stare at her too.

"I present to you, my daughter, Princess Asha, King Runmari," Queen Degnal pronounced.

King Runmari nodded graciously and was pleased that he could look upon mother and daughter both. In his mind, they were quite the astonishing pair. Both were gloriously gorgeous. 'More like sisters,' King Runmari thought and nearly grinned before catching himself. He felt as if he could stare all afternoon at the pair of them. Once again, he envied King Degnal and realized that he was not only incompetent, but also undeserving of such beauty. 'He obviously doesn't even know the real jewels that he has,' thought King Runmari.

"Do you believe it possible that we might come to an arrangement of marriage between your most eligible son and our beloved daughter?" Queen Degnal asked as if it was a command.

King Runmari wanted to shout, 'Yes!' He would have loved nothing more than to be surrounded every day by the likes of them, both mother and daughter. Ever so discreetly, he did manage to nod his head in agreement passively enough as not to convey his excitement at the union. He regretted beyond all hope though that he was in the running for wedding and, most ardently, bedding Asha himself.

CHAPTER 18.

"Close your eyes!" shouted Enithan for the eleventh time.

To Oban's credit, he was sincerely trying to focus, though his mind continued to wander. They had been at it all morning, struggling to concentrate. Both were seated in a very uncomfortable cross-legged position from sun-up to now sundown for seven days straight in what Enithan called 'her garden.' Oban questioned her sanity for calling the dismal grounds anything as beautiful as that. To him, it looked like a dying field of overgrown grass and weeds that had been trampled over by an assortment of heavy-footed wildlife. As he sat with his eyes mostly closed, he couldn't help but think of and, unfortunately, smell the evidence that these roaming beasts left behind. He could also, to his distress, catch periodic whiffs of that same odor coming off his very host and teacher, Enithan. He doubted strongly if she had bathed in many suns or moons.

"Enough of that!" yelled Enithan who he knew could clearly hear his every thought.

Oban turned shamefaced knowing that she knew he found parts of her disturbing, not to mention, stinky. He longed to be with his friends, gloriously breathing fresher air. Yet, he still sat trying to obey Enithan's instructions because he also wished to know more about this mysterious aspect of himself. He deeply desired to know where he fit in the world. He felt utterly lost in his own skin.

"Now, you're thinking like you have some sense," Enithan barked.

Oban didn't know what thought of his appeased Enithan, but he was glad of her seeming positivity.

"Are we ever going to start my training?" asked Oban desperately.

"We could have started a long time ago if you weren't so distracted by everything but this," said Enithan as mildly as she could muster.

Oban frowned at the way Enithan gazed upon him as if he were miserably failing a test.

"You need to be centered in order for me to share with you the ancient secrets," Enithan advised.

At the mentioning of secrets, Oban's ears perked up, and he began giving Enithan his full attention. He tried not to think about nor get upset that she hadn't mentioned that part from the beginning. He quickly shook that minor irritation from his thoughts before she requested yet another day in the overgrown garden.

“We are all too young to even begin to comprehend the evolution of this earth…” she began, “...It is unfathomable to understand its changes, its major alterations that are still taking place even today…” she paused in deep thought before continuing, “...One million winters ago, when the Great Earth was in its infancy, before mankind was a thought, there were elements upon it that possessed enormous power. This energy was everywhere at once emanating from the air, land and at sea. This was when the earth was void of life, and yet it pulsed like a heartbeat of a living creature. Imagine, if you will, a force so great that it breathes like you and I. One might call it a great source, but not at the core of all things for there were gods who created it and gave it its very properties. And, although there are many gods, there is but one who placed mankind to walk upon the earth. He shaped him, them and molded this puny, delicate thing with his own hands, imbuing him with this same might and power that existed everywhere. Legend has it, that he actually placed mankind on earth to rival the other gods,” Enithan said.

She paused again giving Oban an opportunity to let her words sink in. Suddenly, Oban began to have the oddest sensation. He felt as if he were being transported to that very time for which she spoke. He could see liquids and gases hovering over the earth, like clouds that had floated down and were now resting upon it. Still, he stood in his mind's eye in midair wading through the mist in absolute awe of the majesty of what he was witnessing.

"It was he who gave mankind a portion of that very source, that power. During those times, men were like gods bestowed with a touch of those otherworldly characteristics enabling them to accomplish great feats," Enithan smiled at Oban, "There were many gifts, if you will, that were given to man; great strength, speed and agility, a chosen few were bestowed with magic. I heard of some who could even fly. But, we, you and I, are descendants of those with the ability to communicate spirit to spirit, flesh to flesh. We need no language at all. We can enter the very soul of another without them even knowing we're there. Like a thief in the night, we peek in and are gone in a flash," she said.

Oban furrowed his brow.

"What is your question now?" Enithan impatiently asked.

"You know, I do know where babies come from. How can you and I be descendants, when we're not even related?" he asked.

"How naive is this generation?" Enithan asked the air without the slightest inclination of answering Oban.

Instead, she closed her eyes and sighed in exasperation. Eventually, she opened her eyes and simply asked, "Would you like me to continue?"

"Yes…please," Oban replied none too happily on account of her blatant disrespectful nature.

Before Enithan continued, she took a few more deep breaths filled with impatience. Oban knew she could hear his thoughts and resigned himself to refuse to care anymore.

"We all are descendants of the ones who came before us, and if we were to accurately trace back our history to the beginning, we would discover that we are actually kin to one another, more closely knit than some would prefer, but nonetheless, familiar. Mankind evolved to this current state of being, alienation, in a long and winding path, distancing himself not only from his greater family and purpose, but also, unfortunately, from the gods. Alas, the present state of man is separate and apart from his innate, fantastic abilities too. You might ask why, and that would be a very intelligent question. Some say it's because of his appetites; the ones that became more important than his family, his gods. Others would say that it was the natural order of things, that a man should become more independent and cleave to no one. It's not something I spend time pondering. However, this movement towards man's self-reliance has not been beneficial for any of us," she said and paused lost in thought, "Simply put, man thinks he's a god too."

Oban wished she would mull over that one point some more, for he was interested in hearing what else she had to say on the subject.

"As good as we are at glimpsing other's thoughts; our ancestors were even more powerful with the gift. Not only did they know what others were thinking, they were able to plant a thought so seamlessly into someone's mind, that that very person would believe they came up with that thought themselves," she went on.

"Really?" replied Oban.

"Right now, you stumble around clumsily and intrusively, but please note, you hardly know I'm there in yours, do you?" Enithan asked with a smirk.

Oban tried as hard as he could to empty his mind of the thought of choking her at that very moment.

"You need to learn to cloak those thoughts," Enithan

warned, "Especially from someone with an arsenal of weapons like me."

Oban took a deep breath and concentrated on the broken foliage out in front of him.

"Well done, Prince," Enithan smiled, "Well, done."

Despite himself, Oban smiled also realizing that by focusing on something else, it cleared his mind as well.

"I will teach you how to do that without concentrating on anything else," Enithan said.

"Tell me more…please," Oban said, "And, I believe I'm finally ready to learn all you have to teach me."

"Good," Enithan grinned, "Very good. Let's begin."

Enithan stood up and beckoned Oban to do the same. She positioned herself in a stance that reminded Oban of his workouts with his fight instructor.

"Very good," Enithan told him, "It is a fighting stance. Now, you do it."

Oban set his feet apart and bent his knees just as Enithan instructed.

"This is a physical illustration of how your mind and body should be at all times. You need to always be on guard because you do not know if there are threats about," Enithan said, "I need you to tense up your entire being right now. Control yourself; tighten every hair on your head, every part of your body, even your toes."

Then, without warning, Enithan pushed Oban over. Oban crashed down on to the ground.

"Ouch!" Oban exclaimed, "What did you do that for?"

Enithan reached out her hand and helped him back up, "You weren't concentrating enough," she said.

When Oban was on his feet again, Enithan raised her hands to push him down again, but this time Oban was ready for her. He stood as rigid as a tree. She turned and faced another direction then whipped round and tried to push him again. It was to no avail. Oban stood tall and didn't allow her to knock him to the ground again.

"You are a fast learner," Enithan told him, "Notice that your mind is sharper and clearer than it was at first."

"I see a bright light beginning to circle around me," Oban asked, "What is that?"

"A light?" Enithan asked, "Really?"

Oban nodded, yes.

"What color is it?" Enithan asked.

"I think it's yellow," Oban answered.

"Could it be gold?" Enithan asked.

"Yes," Oban said, "It is gold, not yellow. How did you know?"

Enithan looked startled at first. Then she stared at Oban for several moments before regaining her composure.

"It's you in essence. Some say it's your radiance," she paused, "You're beginning to work with your mind, body and spirit," Enithan said, "Up until now, you've only been in one realm of your being, your mind. We need to be connected to all of it and at all times."

As Oban planted his body more stably on the ground, he believed he heard someone say, 'He may even be more powerful than me.' To his surprise, it was Enithan's thought.

That very next morning, unbeknown to the three, Enithan had made arrangements for them to be escorted to Degnal Kingdom. They were awakened by the driver.

"Let's go!" the driver shouted into Enithan's house.

Chinaza, Badu and Oban stepped outside to find a horse drawn cart with a driver waving them into it.

"Where's Enithan?" Oban asked him.

"Who?" the driver asked.

"The lady of this house," Oban answered.

"Oh, her," the driver shrugged, "She told me to take you where you want to go. Now, hurry on. Let's go."

Apparently, Enithan had vanished. When Oban reached in to close the front door, he saw that even her personal items from the house were gone. It was as if she never existed.

"Well, that was strange," Badu giggled.

"I can't wait to leave this place," Chinaza said leaping into the carriage.

Oban jumped up and joined his friends. There was nothing more to say, but he wished he could have simply thanked Enithan. After all, she did save them, and she told him more about his gift than anyone he had ever known. She also informed the driver in great detail where to take them. In a day's ride, Chinaza would be back in Kassel and Badu would be back in his village, and Oban would be back at Degnal Castle.

CHAPTER 19. If Oban were being completely honest, this would be the first time that he had not wished an audience with his father, or even to be near him, for that matter. Sadly, six full moons had passed since his abduction, but the emotional toll made it seem even longer. He felt as if he had aged significantly since their last encounter. The chasm between them was as vast as the Great Sea. In all that time apart, he hadn't received a single word from the King, his once-beloved father. It hurt him deeply even contemplating a reason for the silence. 'What could it be?' he wondered. He could not think of anything resembling justification. What could be more important than the loss of his one and only son?

It didn't help matters that by contrast, his dear sister, Asha, received a cavalry of searchers led by none other, his father, King Degnal. In fact, he swore that no one would rest until she was safely returned. Now, when his son is likewise whisked away to places unknown, in a similarly mysterious manner, Oban is given no consideration whatsoever. 'Why not me?' he asked himself, 'Why not me? Is there something wrong with me?'

"Oban, my son," King Degnal warmly addressed

Oban, actually marveling at the sight of him.

Oban did not return such warmth, but immediately moved coldly across the room as far away from him as he possibly could. King Degnal seemed to take no offense at the deliberate distancing, or at his son recoiling at his attempt to give him a fatherly hug. And, it was clear to King Degnal that Oban would rather lower his countenance to the floor than meet his gaze. King Degnal stepped back a pace clearing acknowledging that his son needed some space. It occurred to him that his once young son was now becoming a man. He tried not to let his smile show by turning aside, but it was too late. Oban had seen the corners of his smile raise.

"My abduction seems to be humorous?" Oban asked probingly.

"I wish it were…" King Degnal began.

"I can see that you do," Oban said turning quickly on his heels and marching toward the exit.

"Wait!" King Degnal shouted.

Oban paused but did not stop. Had it not been for the guards at the door, Oban would have run all the way out of the castle into the open meadows.

"Wait," King Degnal implored.

Oban turned to face him, "What for?"

At that, King Degnal paused and drank from his goblet. Moments later Oban began to distinctly hear his father's voice in his head. It was the oddest thing for Oban. It seemed as if his hearing and his sight had suddenly returned all at once. He looked at his father and saw him as if for the first time since he returned to Degnal. Then he walked over and glanced inside his father's cup. Instinctively, he knew exactly what it was inside.

"Why'd you do that?" Oban asked aloud after hearing in his mind his father's voice saying, 'I took a potion to stop you from hearing my thoughts.'

"Before I tell you why I did it, I have to tell you the whole story from the beginning," King Degnal told him.

"What story?" Oban asked.

"Sit…" King Degnal said, "...please."

At the 'please' Oban went over and sat down obediently. Now that he could hear everything that his father was thinking, he felt less hesitant to do so. What he was gathering from his father's thoughts did not seem encouraging though, however, he felt like he owed his father adequate time to explain. He was beginning to realize that taking a gander at people's thoughts was a complicated endeavor. It appeared to him sometimes like a dream, a most vivid one, and an unraveling tale being presented to him step-by-step. He wished he could encourage his father to think faster so that he could hear it all at once. Alas, that was not the way things worked and he'd have to listen no matter how painstaking this process seemed.

"Of course, you know very well about the 'rite of passage?' King Degnal asked.

"Is that what this was all about?" Oban fumed.

King Degnal sat upon his throne and sighed. He began to take note of all that had happened to his son, and the consequence was his son's hatred of him. The weight of that fact lay heavily upon his heart.

"Now, you have pity for yourself?" Oban asked incredulously, "What about me and what I've been through? Because of you, I was nearly killed at every new sun!"

King Degnal straightened up, noting that his thoughts were not entirely his own. He held back a chuckle as not to offend his son even further.

"No," King Degnal started, "No, son, I certainly don't wish to make any of this about me."

He rose and looked squarely into Oban's eyes, "This is most definitely about you and only you."

"You see, because of your unique ability, I had to go well beyond the traditional rite of passage. Normally, a father would simply prepare his son and have guides and guards stationed at every point…" King Degnal said.

Oban heard all that his father was saying and, to his dismay, everything he was thinking too. Needless to say, he wasn't happy with either.

"...He would even accompany him and make sure that everything went well and according to plan, without interfering, of course, but with you, with you…" King Degnal sighed.

Oban simply continued listening both to his father's thoughts, and words. He had already begun to realize that his great King, father, had many shortcomings. One was that, he left his only son for dead in order to perform some day's old ritual. He was waiting for him to finish his little speech so he could tell him so face-to-face when his father's tone suddenly changed.

"...You are not like everyone else…" King Degnal said admirably, "...You are exceptional; the last one of your kind. The Gods have favored you and therefore the whole of Degnal Kingdom is blessed."

Oban became most attentive with these particular

words intuitively gleaming that this was the true substance of all he had endured thus far. He didn't correct his father either at hearing that he was the last of his kind. Enithan would not be amused if her name was uttered in any context let along an announcement to her King.

"...You are my very own 'thought thief!'" King Degnal said with a broad smile, "...My secret weapon! My precious son," he said and hugged Oban so mightily that he lifted him up and into his arms.

Oban let out a giggle despite his dark mood. King Degnal laughed as well. They both needed that release of tension. Finally, King Degnal painstakingly released Oban and continued. He wished he could hold onto his son forever, and shield him from his fate as Degnal's future King.

"...You see, son, your rite of passage had to be the greatest test, a grand challenge. Your talent needed rigorous assessment beyond its limits...." he paused, "...You would have no idea how completely torturous this was for me. As much as I wanted to, I couldn't intervene. In the eyes of the gods, you had to prove worthy..." King Degnal mournfully cried.

Oban had never seen such emotion coming from his

father. He gathered that they were entering into an uncharted realm of their relationship, something deeper than he'd ever experienced.

"...I need you to forgive me. I had to do it," King Degnal pleaded, "You see that I had to do it. I had no choice!" King Degnal sobbed.

Oban believed his father wholeheartedly. That fact troubled him greatly because he wanted to continue being angry with him.

"...The witch gave me a potion…" he paused, "...I was surprised that it worked so well…" he said soberly, "...The trouble was, it worked so well that it was as if I never had a son…" he paused, filled with regret, "...You see that you must forgive me. You simply must forgive an old fool."

Before Oban knew it, he was at his father's side. All of his defenses were down. He had planned to hate him for the rest of his life. But instead he wrapped his arms around his father's shoulders, knelt down with him and cried. They were both a mess of tears, hugging each other and sobbing uncontrollably.

CHAPTER 20. If Oban were being completely honest, this would be the first time that he had not wished an audience with his father, or even to be near him, for that matter. Sadly, six full moons had passed since his abduction, but the emotional toll made it seem even longer. He felt as if he had aged significantly since their last encounter. The chasm between them was as vast as the Great Sea. In all that time apart, he hadn't received a single word from the King, his once-beloved father. It hurt him deeply even contemplating a reason for the silence. 'What could it be?' he wondered. He could not think of anything resembling justification. What could be more important than the loss of his one and only son?

It didn't help matters that by contrast, his dear sister, Asha, received a cavalry of searchers led by none other, his father, King Degnal. In fact, he swore that no one would rest until she was safely returned. Now, when his son is likewise whisked away to places unknown, in a similarly mysterious manner, Oban is given no consideration whatsoever. 'Why not me?' he asked himself, 'Why not me? Is there something wrong with me?'

"Oban, my son," King Degnal warmly addressed

Oban, actually marveling at the sight of him.

Oban did not return such warmth, but immediately moved coldly across the room as far away from him as he possibly could. King Degnal seemed to take no offense at the deliberate distancing, or at his son recoiling at his attempt to give him a fatherly hug. And, it was clear to King Degnal that Oban would rather lower his countenance to the floor than meet his gaze. King Degnal stepped back a pace clearing acknowledging that his son needed some space. It occurred to him that his once young son was now becoming a man. He tried not to let his smile show by turning aside, but it was too late. Oban had seen the corners of his smile raise.

"My abduction seems to be humorous?" Oban asked probingly.

"I wish it were…" King Degnal began.

"I can see that you do," Oban said turning quickly on his heels and marching toward the exit.

"Wait!" King Degnal shouted.

Oban paused but did not stop. Had it not been for the guards at the door, Oban would have run all the way out of the castle into the open meadows.

"Wait," King Degnal implored.

Oban turned to face him, "What for?"

At that, King Degnal paused and drank from his goblet. Moments later Oban began to distinctly hear his father's voice in his head. It was the oddest thing for Oban. It seemed as if his hearing and his sight had suddenly returned all at once. He looked at his father and saw him as if for the first time since he returned to Degnal. Then he walked over and glanced inside his father's cup. Instinctively, he knew exactly what it was inside.

"Why'd you do that?" Oban asked aloud after hearing in his mind his father's voice saying, 'I took a potion to stop you from hearing my thoughts.'

"Before I tell you why I did it, I have to tell you the whole story from the beginning," King Degnal told him.

"What story?" Oban asked.

"Sit…" King Degnal said, "...please."

At the 'please' Oban went over and sat down obediently. Now that he could hear everything that his father was thinking, he felt less hesitant to do so. What he was gathering from his father's thoughts did not seem encouraging though, however, he felt like he owed his father adequate time to explain. He was beginning to realize that taking a gander at people's thoughts was a complicated endeavor. It appeared to him sometimes like a dream, a most vivid one, and an unraveling tale being presented to him step-by-step. He wished he could encourage his father to think faster so that he could hear it all at once. Alas, that was not the way things worked and he'd have to listen no matter how painstaking this process seemed.

"Of course, you know very well about the 'rite of passage?' King Degnal asked.

"Is that what this was all about?" Oban fumed.

King Degnal sat upon his throne and sighed. He began to take note of all that had happened to his son, and the consequence was his son's hatred of him. The weight of that fact lay heavily upon his heart.

"Now, you have pity for yourself?" Oban asked incredulously, "What about me and what I've been through? Because of you, I was nearly killed at every new sun!"

King Degnal straightened up, noting that his thoughts were not entirely his own. He held back a chuckle as not to offend his son even further.

"No," King Degnal started, "No, son, I certainly don't wish to make any of this about me."

He rose and looked squarely into Oban's eyes, "This is most definitely about you and only you."

"You see, because of your unique ability, I had to go well beyond the traditional rite of passage. Normally, a father would simply prepare his son and have guides and guards stationed at every point…" King Degnal said.

Oban heard all that his father was saying and, to his dismay, everything he was thinking too. Needless to say, he wasn't happy with either.

"...He would even accompany him and make sure that everything went well and according to plan, without interfering, of course, but with you, with you…" King Degnal sighed.

Oban simply continued listening both to his father's thoughts, and words. He had already begun to realize that his great King, father, had many shortcomings. One was that, he left his only son for dead in order to perform some day's old ritual. He was waiting for him to finish his little speech so he could tell him so face-to-face when his father's tone suddenly changed.

"...You are not like everyone else…" King Degnal said admirably, "...You are exceptional; the last one of your kind. The Gods have favored you and therefore the whole of Degnal Kingdom is blessed."

Oban became most attentive with these particular words intuitively gleaming that this was the true substance of all he had endured thus far. He didn't correct his father either at hearing that he was the last of his kind. Enithan would not be amused if her name was uttered in any context let along an announcement to her King.

"...You are my very own 'thought thief!'" King Degnal said with a broad smile, "...My secret weapon! My precious son," he said and hugged Oban so mightily that he lifted him up and into his arms.

Oban let out a giggle despite his dark mood. King Degnal laughed as well. They both needed that release of tension. Finally, King Degnal painstakingly released Oban and continued. He wished he could hold onto his son forever, and shield him from his fate as Degnal's future King.

"...You see, son, your rite of passage had to be the greatest test, a grand challenge. Your talent needed rigorous assessment beyond its limits...." he paused, "...You would have no idea how completely torturous this was for me. As much as I wanted to, I couldn't intervene. In the eyes of the gods, you had to prove worthy..." King Degnal mournfully cried.

Oban had never seen such emotion coming from his father. He gathered that they were entering into an uncharted realm of their relationship, something deeper than he'd ever experienced.

"...I need you to forgive me. I had to do it," King Degnal pleaded, "You see that I had to do it. I had no choice!" King Degnal sobbed.

Oban believed his father wholeheartedly. That fact troubled him greatly because he wanted to continue being angry with him.

"...The witch gave me a potion…" he paused, "...I was surprised that it worked so well…" he said soberly, "...The trouble was, it worked so well that it was as if I never had a son…" he paused, filled with regret, "...You see that you must forgive me. You simply must forgive an old fool."

Before Oban knew it, he was at his father's side. All of his defenses were down. He had planned to hate him for the rest of his life. But instead he wrapped his arms around his father's shoulders, knelt down with him and cried. They were both a mess of tears, hugging each other and sobbing uncontrollably.

CHAPTER 21. Despite all the goings on that day, Asha did finally marry King Runmari's son, Izem. She performed her duties as Princess just as she promised she would continue so with grace and poise. Meanwhile, the two Kings discussed and confirmed all of the details of the union, i.e., where the pair would live, acres of land they'd be given, as well as numbers of servants and field planters, the size of the army they'd have for their protection. No expense would be spared to ensure that things were done fairly and equitably. Asha and Izem would be well taken care of for years to come. There were assurances vowed by both kingdoms to that end.

Asha smiled throughout the ceremony, even when she'd heard from her trusted friend, Guedado, that Ekon had been dispatched directly to prison to await execution. According to Guedado, Ekon would have already been taken care of had it not been Asha's wedding day. Asha felt relieved for his sake. She believed that with time, there was always hope that she might persuade her father to be merciful. She believed she'd be granted that wish as a wedding gift.

Oban exited the winter chamber shortly after the vows had been exchanged. Upon warning his father of Ekon's intentions, he felt saddened about his sister's predicament. More so than anyone else, he knew that Asha was not a very loving sibling but he did feel some affection for her and didn't wish to harm her in any way. He didn't realize that his father had his own suspicions of what really happened to Asha during her absence from the Kingdom. In fact, King Degnal wanted her baby's father to show his face before him just so he could have him run in by his most skilled swordsman. Oban felt that if he had he known his father's desires, he might have warned them both and things could have ended differently. He would have soothed things over for no other reason than to avoid being be related to King Runmari. He didn't trust him still and told his father repeatedly that this seemed like a huge mistake. King Degnal assured him that no one trusted King Runmari and that sometimes enemies needed to be held close. King Degnal would prefer if King Runmari was on his side instead of working against him. For that reason, he wanted to be in a position to keep an eye on him. Oban conceded but promised himself that he wouldn't let his guard down as long as King Runmari was around.

"So, this is where you are," said King Runmari entering the garden where Oban was now standing.

Oban felt that although King Runmari couldn't do what he and Enithan could, he exhibited other equally formidable skills.

"Just needed some air," Oban lied.

Oban quickly realized that he was becoming comfortable with lying.

"Yes. Yes. The air is fresh," noted King Runmari taking a deep breath and closing his eyes.

Oban hoped that would be the extent of their conversation, but knew it wouldn't be.

"I'm very pleased that you passed your challenge," King Runmari said.

"Thank you," Oban replied sincerely.

"No one knew you were being tested so harshly," King Runmari stated, "Had I known, I would have possibly made mention of it so that no harm came your way."

Oban tried to shield himself. He didn't want King Runmari to see the scowl on his face. Too late, King Runmari was apparently very good at interpreting expressions.

"All I want to know is…" King Runmari teased.

Oban did not like this conversation at all. He knew he shouldn't have, but he tensed up, making it difficult for him to hear what King Runmari was thinking.

"I just want to know how is it that you were able to escape so effortlessly each time. Of course, you're trained but you hadn't any weapons, and your only army consisted of a rather round boy and a peevish girl," King Runmari said with a chuckle.

Thankfully, before Oban could come up with a plausible story to tell, his mother, Queen Degnal, approached them in the garden. Oban knew that he had been indeed saved again. Her presence calmed him down immediately.

"Well, I see I'm not the only one in need of air," Queen Degnal said to King Runmari and her son in greeting.

"Yes, mother," Oban nodded.

"Indeed," King Runmari bowed.

The three turned and faced the garden, each in their own thoughts for a moment, just enjoying the scenery. Suddenly, Oban began to feel uneasy again. He tried not to let his panic show, but now that he could clearly hear the thoughts of King Runmari, he became troubled. King Runmari kept repeating one thing: 'Queen Degnal. Queen

Degnal. Queen Degnal.’

End of Part II

Beverly A. Burchett

About the Author

BEVERLY BURCHETT started writing early on in life short stories, plays, poems, and songs. A graduate of the famed High School of Performing Arts, Ms. Burchett has also acted in a number of national commercials as well as a few popular films, including *Fame*, *Joey Breaker,* and she was featured in *The Last O.G.* S3:E2 television series. Her novels are as follows: Queen Kinni, Open Doors, Smart, Sexy, Spiritual, Strong, Random Acts of Kindness, a journey, and the Forgiveness Handbook. She also has a children's book series, called Upside Down and Other Places. This is her latest work, a series entitled: Adventure of a Thought Thief. She's a published songwriter, and member of B.M.I. with works on Jerry *Eastman's Songbook* (album), the theme song for the Annual International Men's Day Conference called *This is What It Means to be a Man*, as well as her own album entitled *Psalm Songs*.

The beginning of Part III

CHAPTER 1. There were no greater builders in all the Great Lands than the clay people in a region known as Olduvai. Their expertise in stone, rocks, and clay earned them that distinct title, though they were also known for many talents and highly coveted secrets. One such secret was how they moved megalithic boulders to erect their towering, intricately built structures. The Olduvais lived in houses that seemed to scrape the very heavens. So much so, the sight of them left visitors in complete wonder. Some in the surrounding villages believed it was easily explainable - slave labor. While others thought - sorcery. Either way, their lands had more advanced living quarters than any other territory. Their forts made their land nearly impenetrable, with walls that were said to reach as high as the stars. This was an exaggeration, but it managed to keep unwanted persons out whilst protecting the citizens within.

Jaiden, Olduvai's King, was a shrewd and cunning leader who took pride in the fact that his people had never been invaded or gone to war with any neighboring territory. This was a rare feat in the lawless, brutal region where he and his people resided. It was one of the safest places in all the Great Lands, even safer than Kenneth, whose year-round winters kept would be marauders at bay. He had just returned from the lavish Degnal wedding of Asha and 'the beast' Izem Runmari. Like his father, King Runmari, Izem was tall, dark, unpleasant and ruthless. He too was in the family business of conquering and pillaging indiscriminately. Practically all who attended the wedding came for one reason only, to witness the disaster for themselves.

No one believed that someone as astute as King Degnal would allow his only daughter to be married to someone like Izem. Everyone knew that the Runmaries would attack anyone in the Great Lands who stood in the way of what they desired. Jaiden attended, same as everyone else, wanting to query King Degnal for his reasoning in orchestrating such a union.

Like everyone else, Jaiden left still pondering that very same question. None of the guests received an answer because King Degnal was tight-lipped throughout the festivities. In fact, other than a minor incident with a young man named Ekon, the ceremony progressed marvelously. Degnal Kingdom was known for its spectacular feasts and this one was the best one yet. The totality of the Kingdom was decorated in silk banners of gold and white announcing the nuptials. Plus, each guest and their families were given quarters for this five-day event, equipped with servants at their beck and call day or night, armed escorts, private chefs and all manner of gifts. King Degnal spared no expense. Even the villagers ate and drank their fill as they camped out surrounding the castle and were given as much as they could stomach from the King's bountiful table.

- **To be continued.**

- on sale now -

www.blackcurrantpress.com
www.amazon.com
www.barnesand noble.com

- Novels -

Queen Kinni

Smart, Sexy, Spiritual, Strong

Random Acts of Kindness

Open Doors

Forgiveness Handbook

Adventures of a Thought Thief, Part I

- Children's Stories -

Upside Down and Other Places

Upside Down and Other Places at Work

Upside Down and Other Places at School

www.ingramcontent.com/pod-product-compliance
Lightning Source LLC
LaVergne TN
LVHW010616100826
845148LV00014B/2991

* 9 7 9 8 9 8 8 2 7 5 4 1 1 *